"Just why do you want this marriage, *signore*?"

"I have a house," Guido replied. "But it is not a home. I have a great name, but no heir. I have relationships, but not with a woman who can fill my heart to the exclusion of all others. Are those good enough reasons?"

Clare looked down her nose. "It all sounds a little cold-blooded to me."

"But you are so wrong," he said softly. "As my wife will discover for herself once I have her in my bed...."

SARA CRAVEN was born in South Devon, England, and grew up surrounded by books, in a house by the sea. After leaving grammar school she worked as a local journalist, covering everything from flower shows to murders. She started writing for Harlequin in 1975. Apart from writing, her passions include films, music, cooking and eating in good restaurants. She now lives in Somerset.

Sara Craven has recently become the latest (and last ever) winner of the British quiz show *Mastermind.*

Sara Craven

BARTALDI'S BRIDE

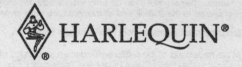

HARLEQUIN®

TORONTO • NEW YORK • LONDON
AMSTERDAM • PARIS • SYDNEY • HAMBURG
STOCKHOLM • ATHENS • TOKYO • MILAN • MADRID
PRAGUE • WARSAW • BUDAPEST • AUCKLAND

ISBN 0-373-12119-9

BARTALDI'S BRIDE

First North American Publication 2000.

Copyright © 1999 by Sara Craven.

This edition published by arrangement with Harlequin Books S.A.

Visit us at www.eHarlequin.com

Printed in U.S.A.

CHAPTER ONE

THE weather in Rome had been swelteringly hot, with clear blue skies and unremitting sunshine, but, as she drove north, Clare could see inky clouds massing over the Appenines and hear a sour mutter of thunder in the distance.

Out of one storm, straight into another, she thought ruefully, urging the hired Fiat round a tortuous bend.

The first storm, however, had been of human origin, and had brought in its wake an abrupt termination to her contracted three months in Italy teaching English to the children of a wealthy Roman family.

And all because the master of the house had a roving eye, and hands to match.

'It is not your fault, *signorina*,' Signora Dorelli, immaculate in grey silk and pearls, had told her that morning, her eyes and mouth steely. 'Do not think that I blame you for my husband's foolish behaviour. You have conducted yourself well. But I should have known better than to bring an attractive young woman into my home.

'At least you may have taught him that he is not irresistible,' she'd added with a shrug. 'But, as things are, I have no choice but to let you go. And the next tutor will be a man, I think.'

So Clare had packed her bags, said a regretful goodbye to the children, whom she'd liked, and expressionlessly accepted the balance of her entire fee, plus a substantial bonus, from a sullen Signor Dorelli, his elegant

Armani suit still stained from the coffee she'd been forced to spill in his lap at breakfast.

If it had been left to him, Clare reflected, she'd have been thrown, penniless, into the street. But fortunately his wife had had other ideas. And no doubt the enforced payment had been only the first stage of an ongoing punishment which could last for weeks, if not months. Signora Dorelli had had the look of a woman prepared to milk the situation for all it was worth.

And he deserves it, Clare told herself. She'd spent a miserable ten days, at first ignoring his lascivious glances and whispered remarks, then doing her damnedest to avoid him physically altogether, thankful that her bedroom door had had a lock on it.

But, however spacious the apartment, she'd not always been totally successful in keeping out of his way, and her flesh crawled as she remembered how he would try to press himself against her in doorways, and the sly groping of his hands whenever he'd caught her alone.

Even his wife's suspicions, expressed at the top of her voice, hadn't been sufficient to deter him.

And when he'd found Clare by herself in the dining room that morning, he'd not only tried to kiss her, but slide a hand up her skirt as well. So Clare, outraged, had poured her coffee over him just as the Signora had entered the room.

Which was why she now found herself free as a bird and driving towards Umbria.

That hadn't been her original plan, of course. Common sense had dictated that she should return to Britain, bank her windfall, and ask the agency to find her another post.

And this she would do—eventually. After she'd been to see Violetta.

A smile curved her lips as she thought of her god-mother, all fluttering hands, scented silks and discreet jewellery. A wealthy widow, who had never been tempted to remarry.

'Why confine yourself to one course, *cara*, when there is a whole banquet to enjoy?' she had once remarked airily.

Violetta, Clare mused, had always had the air of a woman who enjoyed the world, and was treated well by it in return. And, in the heat of the summer, she liked to retire to her charming house in the foothills near Urbino and recuperate from the relentless socialising she embarked on for the rest of the year.

And she was constantly pressing Clare to come and stay with her.

'Come at any time,' she'd told her. 'I so love to see you.' She had wiped away a genuine tear with a lace handkerchief. 'The image of my dearest Laura. My cousin and my greatest friend. How I miss her. And how could your father have put that terrible woman in her place?'

But that was a well-worn path that Clare, wisely, had not chosen to follow.

Laura Marriot had been dead for five years now, and, whatever Clare's private opinion of her stepmother, or the undoubted difficulties of their relationship, Bernice seemed to be making her father happy again, and that was what really counted. Or so she assured herself.

But John Marriot's remarriage had put paid to their cherished plan of Clare joining him as a partner in the successful language school he ran in Cambridge. Bernice had made it clear from the first that this was no longer an option. She wanted no inconvenient reminders of his previous marriage in the shape of a grown-up daughter living close at hand.

Perhaps the physical resemblance to her mother, which was such a joy to Violetta, had been one of the main factors of her resentment.

Every time Bernice had looked at Clare, she'd have seen the creamy skin, the pale blonde hair, the eyes, dark and velvety as pansies, flecked with gold, and the wide mouth that always looked about to break into a smile that Laura had bequeathed to her daughter.

And her possessive streak had been equally unable to handle the closeness between John and Clare. The fact that they were friends as well as father and child.

It had not been easy for Clare to swallow her disappointment and hurt and strike out for herself as a freelance language teacher, but she'd been fortunate in finding, almost at once, her present agency.

Resolutely putting the past behind her, she'd worked with total commitment, accepting each job she was offered without comment or complaint, establishing a track record for reliability and enthusiasm.

The Dorellis had been her first real failure, she acknowledged with a faint sigh.

Now, she felt she deserved a short break before plunging into another assignment. It was nearly two years since she'd had a holiday, and at her godmother's house she'd be petted and cherished in a way she hadn't known for years. It was a beguiling thought.

A more ominous rumble of thunder made her glance skywards, grimacing slightly. She was still miles from Cenacchio, where Violetta lived, and there was little chance of outrunning the storm. She knew how fierce and unpredictable the weather could suddenly become in this region.

Even as the thought formed, the first raindrops hurled themselves against her windscreen. Seconds later, they'd become a deluge with which the Fiat's wipers were clearly reluctant or unable to cope.

Not conditions for driving on unfamiliar roads with severe gradients, Clare decided, prudently pulling over on to a gravelled verge. She couldn't beat the storm, but she could sit it out.

She'd bought some cartons of fruit juice at the service station where she'd stopped for lunch, and petrol. Thankfully, she opened one of the drinks, and felt its chill refresh her dry mouth.

The rain was like a curtain, sweeping in great swathes across her vision. She watched the lightning splitting the sky apart, then zig-zagging down to lose itself in the great hills which marched down the spine of Italy. The thunder seemed to echo from peak to peak.

Son et lumière at its ultimate, thought Clare, finishing her drink. She leaned forward to get a tissue to wipe her fingers, and paused, frowning. Impossible as it might seem, she would swear she had just seen signs of movement straight ahead through the barrage of rain.

Surely not, she thought incredulously. No one in their right mind would choose to walk around in weather like this.

She peered intently through the windscreen, realising she hadn't been mistaken. Someone was coming towards her along the road. A girl's figure, she realised in astonishment, weighed down by a heavy suitcase, and limping badly too.

Clare wound down her window. As the hobbling figure drew level, she said in Italian, 'Are you in trouble? May I help?'

The girl hesitated. She was barely out of adolescence,

and stunningly pretty in spite of the dark hair which hung in drowned rats' tails round her face, and an understandably peevish expression.

She said, 'Please do not concern yourself, *signora*. I can manage very well.'

'That's not how it seems to me,' Clare returned levelly. 'Have you hurt your ankle?'

'No.' The sulky look deepened. 'It's the heel of this stupid shoe—see? It broke off.'

Clare said crisply, 'If you plan to continue your stroll, I suggest you snap the other one off, and even things up a little.'

'I am not taking a stroll,' the younger girl said haughtily. 'I was driving a car until it ran out of petrol.'

Clare's brows lifted. 'Are you old enough to drive?' she asked, mindful that Italian licences were only issued to over-eighteen-year-olds.

There was a betraying pause, then, 'Of course I am.' The girl made a face like an aggravated kitten. 'It is just that the car never has a full tank in case I run away.'

Clare gave the suitcase a thoughtful glance. 'And isn't that precisely what you're doing?'

The girl tried to look dignified as well as drenched. 'That, *signora*, is none of your business.'

'Then I'm going to make it my business.' Clare opened the passenger door invitingly. 'At least shelter with me until it stops raining, otherwise you're going to catch pneumonia.'

'But I do not know you,' the other objected. 'You could be—anybody.'

'I can assure you that I'm nobody. Nobody that matters, anyway.' Clare's voice was gentle. 'And I think you'd be safer in this car than out on the open road.'

The girl's eyes widened. 'You think I could be struck by lightning?'

'I think that's the least that could happen to you,' Clare told her quietly. 'Now, put your case in the back of the car and get in before you drown.'

As the newcomer slid into the passenger seat, Clare could see she was shivering. Her pale pink dress, which undoubtedly bore the label of some leading designer, was pasted to her body, and the narrow strappy shoes that matched it were discoloured and leaking as well as lop-sided.

Clare reached into the back of the car and retrieved the raincoat she'd thrown there a few hours before. She'd left the Dorellis in such a hurry that she'd almost forgotten it, and their maid had chased after her waving it.

She said, 'You need to get out of that wet dress. If you put this on and button it right up, no one will notice anything.' She paused. 'I'm afraid I can't offer you anything hot to drink, but there's some fruit juice if you'd like it.'

There was an uncertain silence. Then, 'You are kind.'

Clare busied herself opening the carton, tactfully ignoring the wriggling and muttered curses going on beside her.

'My dress it ruined,' the girl announced after a moment or two. 'It will have to be thrown away.'

Clare swallowed. 'Isn't that rather extravagant?' she asked mildly.

'It does not matter.' The girl shrugged, pushing the pile of crumpled pink linen away with a bare foot.

'What about your car?' Clare handed over the drink. 'Where did you leave that?'

Another shrug. 'Somewhere.' A swift, sideways glance. 'I do not remember.'

'What a shame,' Clare said drily. 'Perhaps we'd better introduce ourselves. 'I'm Clare Marriot.'

The girl stared at her. 'You are English? But your Italian is good. I was deceived.'

Clare smiled. 'My mother was Italian, and it's one of the languages I teach.'

'Truly? What are the others?'

'Oh, French, Spanish—a little German. And English itself, of course.'

'Is that why you are here—to teach English?'

Clare shook her head. 'No, I'm on holiday.' She paused. 'What's your name?'

'It is Paola—Morisone.'

Again, the brief hesitation wasn't lost on Clare.

But she didn't query it. Instead, she said, 'It looks as if the storm could be passing. If you'll tell me where you live, I'll take you home.'

'No.' The denial was snapped at her. 'I do not go home—not now, not ever.'

Clare groaned inwardly. She said quietly, 'Be reasonable. You're soaked to the skin, and your shoe is broken. Besides, I'm sure people will be worried about you.'

Paola tossed her head. 'Let them. I do not care. And if Guido thinks I am dead, then it is good, because he will not try to make me marry him any more.'

Clare stared at her, trying to unravel the strands of this pronouncement and absorb its implications at the same time.

She said 'Guido?'

'My brother. He is a pig.'

Clare felt dazed. 'Your brother?' Her voice rose. 'But that's absurd. You can't...'

'Oh, he is not a real brother.' Paola wrinkled her nose dismissively. 'My father and his were in business together, and when my father died, Zio Carlo said I must live with him.' Her face darkened. 'Although I did not want to. I wished to stay with my *matrigna*, and she wished it too, but the lawyers would not permit it.'

At least Paola seems to have had more luck with her stepmother than I did, Clare thought, wryly. Bernice couldn't wait to get me out of the house. But she had other problems.

She said, feeling her way. 'And is it Zio Carlo's wish that you should marry this Guido?'

'*Dio*, no. He is also dead.' Paola heaved a sigh. 'But he said in his will that Guido should be my guardian until I am twenty-five, which is when my money comes to me. Unless I am married before that, of course. Which I mean to be. Although not to Guido, whom I hate.'

Clare felt as if she was wading through linguine. She took a deep breath. 'Aren't you rather young to be thinking about marriage—to anyone?'

'I am eighteen—or I shall be very soon,' she added, returning Clare's sceptical glance with a mutinous glare. 'And my own mother was my age when she met my father and fell in love.' She made a sweeping, impassioned gesture, nearly spilling the remains of her drink. 'When you meet the one man in the world who is for you, nothing else matters.'

'I see,' Clare said drily, taking the carton and putting it out of harm's way. 'And have you met such a man?'

'Of course. His name is Fabio.' Paola's eyes shone. 'And he is wonderful. He is going to save me from Guido.'

It was all delicious nonsense, Clare thought, half-amused, half-exasperated. But it was also full time to introduce a note of reality.

She said, 'Paola—it's nearly the twenty-first century. People stopped forcing others into marriage a long time ago. If Guido knows how you really feel...'

'He does not care. It is the money—only the money. My father's share in the business belongs to me. If I marry someone else, it will be lost to him. He will not permit that. For three years he has kept me in prison.'

'Prison?' Clare echoed faintly. 'What are you talking about?'

Paola's delicate mouth was set sullenly. 'He made me go to this school. The nuns were like jailers. He did this so I could not meet anyone else and be happy.'

It occurred to Clare that the unknown Guido might have a point. Paola clearly had all the common sense of a butterfly.

But that didn't mean he should be allowed to pressure such an immature girl into matrimony for mercenary reasons, she reminded herself. If that was what he was actually doing.

She said gently, 'Perhaps he really loves you, Paola, and wants to take care of you.'

Paola made a contemptuous noise. 'I do not believe that. He is concerned for his business—for losing control of my share. That is all.'

'Oh.' Clare digested this, then started on a different tack. 'How did you meet Fabio?'

'I was on holiday,' Paola said dreamily. 'At Portofino with my friend Carlotta and her family. Guido let me go there because Carlotta's mother is just as strict as the nuns.' She giggled. 'But Carlotta and I used to climb out of the window at the villa, and go into the town at night. One time, we were at a disco, when some men tried to get fresh with us, so Fabio and his friend came to help us.' She sighed ecstatically. 'I looked at him—and I knew. And it was the same for him.'

'How fortunate,' Clare said slowly. 'And you've—kept in touch ever since?'

Paola nodded eagerly. 'He writes to me, and I pretend the letters are from Carlotta.'

'You haven't told Guido about this boy?'

'Are you crazy?' Paola cast her eyes to heaven. 'Do you know what he would do? Send me to another prison—in Switzerland—so that I learn to cook, and arrange flowers, and be a hostess. For him,' she added venomously.

She paused. 'And Fabio is not a boy. He is a man, although not as old as Guido, naturally. And far more handsome.' She rolled her eyes. *'Bello, bello.'*

An image of Guido as an ageing lecher, on the lines of the loathsome Signor Dorelli, lodged in Clare's mind. She could well understand Fabio's appeal, yet, at the same time, she was aware of all kinds of nameless worries.

She said, probing gently, 'And is that where you're going now? To meet Fabio somewhere?'

Paola nodded vigorously. *'Si*—and to be married.'

Don't get involved, said a small voice of sanity in the back of Clare's brain. Just take her to the nearest service station, and then get on with your own life. This has nothing to do with you.

She said, 'Where is the wedding taking place?'

Paola shrugged. 'I do not know. Fabio is making all the arrangements.'

Clare looked at her thoughtfully. By her own admission, Paola was barely more than a child, she thought ruefully, yet here she was—about to jump out of the frying pan into the fire.

This Guido sounded none too savoury, but she had even less time for Fabio, persuading a young and vulnerable girl, who also happened to be an heiress, into a runaway marriage.

'And where are you meeting him?'

'In Barezzo—at the rail station.' Paola gave a fretful look at the delicate platinum watch she was wearing. 'I shall be late. He will be angry with me.'

'Are you catching a particular train?'

'No—it is just a good place to meet, because there will be many other people doing the same, and Fabio says no one will notice us.'

The more she heard of these arrangements, the less Clare liked them.

She said drily, 'He seems to have it all worked out.'

'But of course.' Paola began to hunt through her elegant kid purse. 'He wrote to me telling me exactly what I must do. I have his letter—somewhere. Only, if I am late, it will ruin everything.' Paola paused, directing a speculative look at Clare. 'Unless, *signorina*, you would drive me to Barezzo.'

Clare hardened her heart against the coaxing tone and winning smile.

She said, 'I'm afraid I'm going in a different direction.'

'But it would not take you long—and it would help me so much.' Paola laid a pleading hand on her arm.

'But you have a car of your own. I'll help you get petrol for it and...'

'No, that would take too long. I must get to Barezzo before she realises I am gone, and starts to look for me.'

'She?' Clare was losing the plot again.

'The Signora. The woman Guido employs to watch me when he is not there.'

'Does that happen often?'

'*Sì*. He is away now, and I am left with her. She is a witch,' Paola said passionately. 'And I hate her.'

Not a very competent witch, Clare thought drily, or she'd have looked into her crystal ball and sussed exactly what her charge was up to.

'But Guido will return soon—perhaps tomorrow—and try to make me marry him again, so this may be my last chance to escape.' Paola shivered dramatically. 'He frightens me.'

Clare's mouth tightened, as the memory of Signor Dorelli returned. She said slowly, 'Just what kind of pressure does he put on you?'

'You mean does he make love to me?' Paola shook her head. 'No, he is always cold. I think I am too young for him.' She gave Clare a sideways worldly look that she had not learned from the nuns. 'Besides, he has a woman already. She lives in Sienna.'

It just gets worse and worse, Clare thought, frowning.

She took a deep breath. 'Even so, I really think it would be best for you to stop and consider what you're doing before you leap into this other marriage. After all, you hardly know Fabio, and holiday romances rarely last the distance...'

'You want me to go home,' Paola accused. 'Back to that prison. And I will not. If you will not drive me, then I will walk to Barezzo,' she added, reaching for the damp pink dress.

'No, you won't,' Clare said wearily. 'I'll drive you.'

Perhaps, on the way, she could talk some sense into her companion, she thought, without optimism. Or at least warn her gently about the handsome young men who hung round fashionable resorts on the look-out for rich women.

And Paola had the additional advantages of being very young and extremely pretty.

Fabio must have thought it was his birthday, Clare thought with an inward sigh, as she started the car.

She was still trying to work out the most tactful approach when she realised that Paola had fallen deeply and peacefully asleep.

The rain had stopped, and the sun was trying to make belated amends when they reached Barezzo about half an hour later.

Clare parked outside the station, and looked round her. She hadn't visited Barezzo before, but its main square seemed pleasant, with a central fountain, and an enormous church dominating all the buildings round it.

She leaned towards Paola, and spoke her name quietly, but the younger girl did not stir.

But maybe this is for the best, she thought. It gives me a chance to have a look at this guy—ask a few questions. Let him know that I'm aware of what he's up to.

She had no idea why she should be taking all this trouble for a girl who was still a virtual stranger, despite her airy confidences. Except that Paola seemed to need a friend.

And I'm all there is, she told herself, as she left the car.

Contrary to Paola's expectations, the station wasn't crowded with latter-day Romeos passionately greeting their Juliets.

In fact, the concourse was all but deserted, the sole exception being a man casually leaning against a stone pillar.

He had the air of someone who'd been there for a

while, and was prepared to wait all day if necessary, Clare thought as she walked towards him, her sandals clicking on the marble floor. So, presumably, this had to be Fabio.

As she neared him, he straightened slowly, like some great cat preparing to pounce, she realised, finding her breath fluttering unevenly as she took her first good look at him.

My God, she thought ironically, but with reluctant appreciation, as she halted a deliberate few feet away from him. Sex on legs.

And such long legs too, she noted, covered in well-cut and expensive trousers. His casual shirt was navy and unbuttoned at the throat, and a jacket that had to be the work of a top designer hung from his broad shoulders.

It was clear why he needed a wealthy wife. It would probably take everything Paola possessed to keep him in the manner he considered his due.

He was in his mid-thirties, she judged, and around six foot tall, his black glossy hair reaching almost to his collar in tousled chic.

But he wasn't conventionally handsome, she decided critically, although he had cheekbones to die for. The dark, brilliant eyes, now fixed on her with equal interest, were too heavy-lidded, and his nose and chin too strongly marked. But any impression of austerity was belied by his mouth, firm-lipped yet unashamedly sensuous.

Which wasn't all. There was an effortless confidence about him—an impression of power barely reined in—that she found physically disturbing.

Power, she found herself thinking. The ultimate aphrodisiac...

No wonder Paola, freed from the restrictions of her convent school, had been swept off her feet with such ease.

Men like this should carry a government warning, Clare told herself grimly.

She said in Italian, 'Are you waiting for Paola, *signore*?'

'*Si, signorina.*' His voice was low and resonant, his tone courteous, but Clare was sharply aware of a subtle change in his stance. A new tension. There was still a safe distance between them, so it was foolish to feel menaced, but she did.

The notion that here was a tiger on a leash became conviction. This, she realised shakily, was a determined and dangerous man, and what the hell was she doing crossing swords with him? Except that Paola needed to be protected, she reminded herself swiftly.

The dark eyes were fixed on her. 'Do you know where she is?'

'Naturally,' Clare said. 'But I wanted to talk to you about her first.'

He said softly, 'Ah. And you are…?'

'That doesn't matter,' she said quickly.

'I think it does.' His dark gaze was charged now, taking in every detail from the top of her head to the soles of her feet. She saw his mouth curl slightly, and was vexed to find that she minded.

After all, what possible interest could she have for him in her chainstore dress and sandals? She derided herself. She was a working girl, not the kind of rich child he needed to stalk.

And, heaven knows, he was the last type of man that she'd ever want to be involved with anyway. So, what was her problem?

He said, 'You're not what I was expecting.'

Clare lifted her chin. 'I was thinking the same about you.'

He inclined his head almost mockingly. 'That I can believe,' he murmured. 'So—where is Paola?'

'She's perfectly safe.'

'I am relieved to hear it.' The dark gaze seemed to burn into hers. 'May I see her?'

'Of course.' Clare nodded, conscious of a faint bewilderment. Even unease. 'But before that, we really need to talk.'

He was smiling at her. 'Oh, you will talk, *signorina*. But not to me.'

He made a slight gesture with his hand, and Clare became suddenly aware of movement beside her—behind her. Men in uniform appearing as if from nowhere. Men with guns which—dear God—they were pointing at her.

She felt her arms taken, dragged behind her back. Felt, as she began to struggle, handcuffs snapped on to her wrists. She wanted to scream a protest, but her taut throat wouldn't utter a sound.

All she could do was look back at her adversary with dazed horror as an excited babble of sound ebbed and flowed around her.

She said hoarsely, 'Who are you?'

'I am Guido Bartaldi, *signorina*. And you are one of the creatures who has kidnapped my ward.' His voice cut into her like the lash of a whip. 'Now tell me what you have done with her.'

'Kidnapped?' Clare's voice rose to a shriek. 'Are you mad?'

The sudden surprised silence, and the expression of

frowning incredulity on Guido Bartaldi's face alerted her
to the fact that she'd spoken in English.

'You are the mad one,' he returned in the same language. 'To think that you and your accomplice could get
away with this.'

'I have no accomplice.' Reaction was setting in, and
Clare was suddenly shaking. Her eyes searched the dark,
inimical face pleadingly. 'I met Paola on the road, and
gave her a lift—that's all.'

'Marchese.' A policeman hurried up. 'The little one
is outside in a car. She is unconscious—drugged, I
think—but she is alive.'

'She's asleep, not drugged,' Clare said desperately,
the word 'Marchese' echoing in her brain. Paola had
failed to mention that her unwanted bridegroom was a
marquis.

'See that she is taken to the local clinic at once,' the
Marchese ordered curtly. His dark eyes seared Clare. 'As
for this one—get her out of my sight—now.'

Her arms were held, and she was turned not gently
towards the exit.

'Please,' she flung back over her shoulder. 'You're
making a terrible mistake.'

'The mistake is yours, *signorina*.' His tone was harsh.
'But you will pay dearly for it, I promise you.'

And he turned his back in icy dismissal.

CHAPTER TWO

IT WAS a small room she was taken to, with one high, barred window, a table and chairs. On the table there was a plastic bottle of mineral water, and a paper cup.

So that I don't seize the opportunity to slash my wrists, Clare thought, biting her lip.

But at least they hadn't put her in a cell—or at least not yet. And, thankfully, they'd removed the handcuffs.

The afternoon heat was turning the room into an oven, but she was shivering just the same.

Two men in plain clothes, their faces unsmiling, had asked her some preliminary questions. She'd given her name, age and occupation, and her reason for being in Italy. They had asked where she had been staying, and she'd told them Rome. But she'd hesitated when they'd requested the name and address of her hosts there. Neither of the Dorellis, after all, had any reason to wish her well. She could just imagine the smile of oily triumph on the Signore's face if he learned she'd been arrested.

But she knew that her refusal to answer had been another black mark against her. After that, she'd been left alone.

Fabio had not been mentioned, although she was sure that he was the accomplice the Marchese had referred to.

What on earth had he done? she wondered. After all, planning an elopement was hardly a criminal offence.

Although running off with the Marchese Bartaldi's in-

23

tended wife could well be considered a capital crime, she acknowledged, her mouth twisting. She'd seen the deference with which he was treated.

Guido Bartaldi, she thought. The name was familiar, but, for the life of her, she didn't know why. Her tired, scared brain refused to make the connection.

All she could be sure of was that she had never, in her life—in her wildest dream or worst nightmare—encountered Guido Bartaldi in person before.

That I could never have forgotten, she told herself grimly. His lean hawk's face with the shadowed, contemptuous eyes seemed to burn in her mind.

Paola had said he was cold, but he was worse than that. He was ice—he was marble. He was darkness.

But it was no use sitting there hating him.

I must think, she told herself, straightening her shoulders and resisting an impulse to put her head down on the table and weep with weariness and fright. So far I've let everyone else call the shots. I need to phone the British Consul and tell Violetta as well. I don't want to worry my father unless it becomes strictly necessary.

But it won't come to that, she tried to reassure herself. Paola has to have woken up by now, so they must know I'm innocent.

Unless she's too scared to tell them the truth, she thought apprehensively, her stomach churning. Unless she decides to pretend she was abducted rather than admit she was running away. Oh, dear God, she could just do that.

She also wished she knew more about the Italian legal system, and how it worked, but she'd never needed to before. Should she have asked for a lawyer right away? she wondered. Violetta was bound to know a good one.

She also wished she knew what the time was, but they'd taken her watch, as well as her handbag.

I seem to have been here for hours, she thought.

Her shoulders ached with tension, and her clothes felt as if they were pasted to her damp body. It was hard to raise her spirits and try and think logically when she was, physically and mentally, at such a low ebb.

She heard the sound of a key in the lock, and her whole body went rigid as she stared at the door. What now?

To her surprise, the Marchese Bartaldi walked into the room. He paused, staring at her, the dark eyes narrowed, his mouth grim and set.

She was immediately and startlingly aware of the scent of him, a compound of some faint, expensive cologne, clean male skin, and fresh linen. An evocative mix that stamped its presence on the heavy atmosphere.

Angrily aware that she was trembling inside, but determined to make a show of resistance, Clare pushed back her chair and got slowly to her feet, forcing herself to return his gaze.

At the same time she registered that he was carrying her bag, which he tossed negligently on to the table between them. Some of its contents—her passport, car keys and wallet—spilled out on to the polished wood. The casual, almost contemptuous actions ignited a small flame of temper deep within her. What was he doing handling her things? He wasn't a policeman.

But he was a rich and powerful man, she thought, feeding her own contempt. Maybe he had the local police force in his pocket.

He said, in English, 'Please sit down.'

Clare put her hands behind her back. 'I prefer to stand.'

'As you wish.' He paused, looking her over from head to foot, his glance measured, even appraising.

Lifting her chin, she endured his scrutiny in silence, bitterly aware that she must look an overheated, bedraggled mess.

Not that it mattered. She wasn't out to make any kind of feminine appeal to him. As far as he was concerned, she'd already been tried and condemned.

He said, 'Be good enough, *signorina*, to tell me exactly how you and my ward came to encounter each other.'

'I would prefer to tell the British Consul,' Clare said icily. 'I also wish to make a telephone call to my godmother, and be provided with a lawyer.'

He sighed. 'One thing at a time, Miss Marriot. Firstly, why was Paola in your car?'

'How many more times do I have to say it?' Clare asked mutinously. 'I was driving to my godmother's house at Cenacchio and got caught in the storm.'

'Your godmother is whom?'

'Signora Andreati at the Villa Rosa.'

He nodded. 'I have heard of her.'

'I'm sure she'll be overwhelmed.'

His mouth tightened. 'I advise you to keep a civil tongue in your head.'

'Oh, I'm sorry,' Clare said. 'Am I not behaving with sufficient deference, Marchese? It must be a new experience for you.'

'The whole situation is one I am not anxious to repeat.' His tone bit. 'Please go on with your story.'

Clare sighed. 'I found Paola on the road, soaked to the skin. She seemed vulnerable, and her story worried me, so I decided to help. She persuaded me to drive her to the station, but when we arrived she was asleep, so I thought I'd have a look at this Fabio for myself. Get rid of him, if I could.'

She shrugged. 'You were waiting, so I assumed you were Fabio.'

'I am not flattered by the mistake,' he said coldly.

'Oh, allow me to apologise,' Clare said scornfully. 'I, of course, have had a thrilling bloody afternoon. Accused of kidnapping, arrested by armed guards, interrogated, and locked into this oven. Absolutely ideal—wouldn't you say?'

'Perhaps it will teach you in future not to meddle in situations which do not concern you,' Guido Bartaldi said grimly. He paused. 'But you will be pleased to know that Paola is awake, and confirms your story.'

'Really?' Clare raised her eyebrows.

The firm mouth tightened. 'You seem surprised, *signorina*. Not a reassuring reaction.'

'I am surprised,' Clare's tone was dry. 'Paola didn't strike me as a great friend to truth. I thought she'd say whatever was needed to show her in a good light.'

His brows snapped together ominously, and Clare stared at the floor, waiting for the thunderbolt to strike. Instead, there was a brief taut silence, then, incredibly, a low, amused chuckle.

'You seem a shrewd judge of character, *signorina*,' the Marchese drawled, as her startled gaze met his.

She shrugged. 'It hardly needs a degree in psychology to know that Paola's a girl who'll react unpredictably, even dangerously, if pushed into a corner.' She added deliberately, 'Also, when she's bored, she'll look for mischief. She is, after all, very young. You're going to have your hands full,' she added with a certain satisfaction.

'I am obliged for your assessment.' There was a faint

note of anger in the quiet voice. 'But I am quite capable of making the appropriate arrangements for her welfare.'

'Which is why she was trying to run away with some smooth-talking crook, I suppose.' Clare paused. 'Incidentally, what became of Fabio? Is he in the next cell?'

Guido Bartaldi shook his head. 'He has not been arrested.'

'I see,' Clare said unsteadily. 'That privilege was reserved for me.'

He said coldly, 'You were arrested, *signorina*, because the police were not convinced that Fabio was working alone, and your ill-timed arrival gave credence to their suspicions. That is all that happened.'

Clare gasped indignantly. 'Clearly you think I got off lightly.'

'If you had been involved, it would have been the worse for you.' The words were spoken softly, but Clare felt the hairs stand up on the back of her neck.

She tilted her chin. 'It doesn't worry you that I could sue for false arrest?'

'When you walked into the station, I did not know what part you were playing. And I could not take any chances. My sole concern in this matter has been for Paola.'

'Well, I suppose that's something,' Clare said with a touch of austerity, recalling what Paola had told her of the woman he visited in Siena. Perhaps today's incident might have made him revise his feelings, she thought. Might even have convinced him that he was fonder of Paola than he realised.

She found herself frowning slightly. 'So, where is Fabio?'

The Marchese shrugged elegant shoulders. 'Who

knows? He had the audacity to telephone me and ask how much I would pay him not to marry Paola.'

Clare winced. 'Poor Paola.'

'He believed, you see, that I did not know where to find her, and would be frantic to get her back on any terms.'

'How did you know?' Clare's curiosity got the better of her.

He shrugged again. 'Unfortunately for him, Paola had left his letter detailing all the arrangements in her bedroom.'

In spite of weariness, strain and anger, Clare's mouth curved into an involuntary smile. 'Oh, no. Surely not.'

'She is not a very experienced conspirator,' the Marchese conceded sardonically. 'When he realised that I knew the time and place of their rendezvous, he decided it was better to be discreet than brave, and rang off in a great hurry.' He paused. 'I went to collect Paola—and instead I found you,' he added softly.

'Yes, you did.' Clare gave him a defiant stare. 'And, even if it was interference, I'm still glad I didn't just abandon her.'

'Would you believe that I am glad too? Even grateful?'

'Oh, please don't go overboard,' Clare begged sarcastically. She hesitated. 'What will happen to Fabio? Are you going to pursue him? Charge him with something?'

The Marchese shook his head. 'He was not a serious kidnapper. Just an unpleasant leech who saw a chance to make himself some easy money at my expense. I imagine it is not the first time he has been paid to go away.'

'But this time he misjudged his opponent.' Clare's tone was ironic.

'As you say.'

'Congratulations, *signore*. I hope next time you don't have to mount a full-scale operation to stop Paola running away.'

'There will not be a next time,' he said curtly. 'I believed she was sufficiently protected. However, I was wrong, and other steps will have to be taken.'

'Not the school in Switzerland, I trust,' Clare said before she could stop herself.

The dark eyes raked her. 'She seems to have taken you fully into her confidence.'

Clare met his gaze steadily. 'Sometimes it's easier to talk to a stranger. Someone you'll never see again.' She paused. 'Talking of which, I hope I'm free to go now.'

'Of course.'

'Oh, I'm taking nothing for granted.' *Not until I've put at least a hundred kilometres between us,* she added silently.

'I regret that your vacation has been interrupted so unpleasantly. Do you intend to journey on to Cenacchio?'

'I'm not sure what my plans are,' Clare said guardedly. Whatever, she wasn't prepared to share them, especially with an Italian aristocrat who seemed to regard the rest of creation as so many puppets to dance to his tug on the strings.

He picked up her bag and replaced the items that had fallen out, with the exception of her passport, which he opened and studied for a moment.

Then he looked at her, his lips twisting in a faint smile. He said softly, 'Your photograph does not do you justice—Chiara.'

It had been a long time since anyone had used the Italian version of her name. Not since her mother...

Clare bit her lip hard, staring rigidly at the table.

There'd been an odd note in his voice, she realised. Something disturbing—even sensuous—that had prickled along her nerve-endings.

'Would you like to see Paola?' he went on in the same quiet tone. 'I am sure she would wish to thank you.'

The walls of the room seemed to be contracting strangely, startling her with a sudden vivid awareness of his proximity to her. A troubling certainty that she was in more danger now than she had been all day. Or even ever before.

She thought, I've got to get out of here—away from here...

She forced a stiff little smile. 'I'd prefer to leave things as they are. Please tell her I said goodbye—and good luck,' she added deliberately. 'I think she's going to need it.'

He smiled back at her. 'Oh, I think we all make our own good fortune—don't you?'

'I—I haven't given it much thought.' She put out her hand. 'May I have my bag, please?'

For an uneasy moment she was sure he was going to make her reach out and take it from him.

But he passed it across the table to her without comment. He had good hands, she noted without pleasure, with square, capable palms and long fingers. Strong, powerful hands. But, she wondered, could they also be gentle...?

She caught herself hastily. She couldn't afford to indulge in that kind of speculation. It simply wasn't safe.

Guido Bartaldi wasn't safe, she thought, making a play of checking the contents of her bag.

'You will find everything there.' He sounded amused.

'As I said, I'm taking nothing for granted.' She found her watch, and fastened it back on to her wrist, her fingers clumsy with haste as she struggled with the clasp.

'May I help?'

'No—no, thank you,' she said hastily. The thought of him touching her, even in such a brief asexual contact, was enough to bring warm colour into her face. She kept her head bent as she completed the fastening.

And then something else in her bag attracted her attention, and she stiffened.

'Just a moment.' She extracted an envelope. 'This isn't mine.'

'Open it.'

The envelope contained money—lira notes in large denominations. Getting on for a thousand pounds, she thought numbly.

She looked up and met his expressionless gaze. She said, 'What is this? Some kind of set-up?'

'On the contrary,' he returned. 'Let us call it a tangible expression of my regret for the inconvenience you have suffered.'

'Of course,' she said. 'The rich man's solution for everything. Throw money at it.'

'I had hoped,' he said, 'that it might make you look more kindly on me.'

Clare shook her head. 'I'm sorry, *signore*.' She kept her voice clipped and cool. 'You may have bought the local police force, but my goodwill isn't for sale. Not now. Not ever.'

The notes tore quite easily. As Guido Bartaldi watched her, motionless and silent, Clare ripped them across, and across, reducing them savagely to the most expensive confetti in the world, then tossing the fragments into the air.

She said, 'Consider all debts cancelled, Marchese,' then she walked swiftly round the table and past him to the door. The handle was slippery in her damp hand, but she managed to twist it and get the door open.

At any moment she was expecting him to stop her physically from leaving. Waiting for his anger to strike her like lightning over the Appenines. Apart from anything else, defacing a national currency was probably some kind of offence.

But there wasn't a sound behind her, or a movement. Only a stillness and a silence that was ominous in its totality. That followed her like a shadow. But ahead of her was another open door and a sunlit street, and she kept walking, trying not to break into a run.

'Signorina.' An officer came out of one of the offices that lined the corridor, and she swung round in panic, feeling a scream rising in her throat, until she realised he was simply telling her where her car was parked.

She managed to choke out a word of thanks, and went on, aware of curious glances following her.

She found the little Fiat, and got in to the driving seat. For a moment, she stared blindly ahead of her through the windscreen, then she bent and put her head down on the steering wheel, and let the inevitable storm of weeping that had been building steadily over the past hour exorcise her shock and fright.

When it was over, she dried her eyes on a handful of tissues, put on some more lipstick, and started the car. The sooner she got on with her life and put today's shambles out of her mind the better.

But it wasn't so easy to do. She found she was constantly glancing in the mirror, her heart thumping each time a car came up behind her.

You're being ridiculous, she told herself. It's all over. You'll never see him again.

So, why, in spite of the distance between them, was she conscious of his presence like the touch of a hand on her skin? And his voice saying softly, 'Chiara'?

'Mia cara.' Violetta's voice was like warm honey. 'What a nightmare for you. Now, tell me everything. You were actually imprisoned?'

They were sitting in the *salone*, with the shutters drawn to exclude the late-afternoon sun, drinking the strong black coffee which Violetta consumed at all hours of the day and night and eating some little almond cakes.

'Well, not in a cell,' Clare admitted. The warmth and exuberance of her welcome both from her godmother and Angelina, her plump, smiling housekeeper, had been just what she'd needed to heal the wounds of the day. And, now, sitting in this calm, gracious room, able to pour her story into loving, sympathetic ears, she could feel the tension seeping out of her.

'But it felt as bad.' She shuddered. 'I didn't know what to do. I couldn't think properly. I realise now why people confess to things they haven't done.' She frowned darkly. 'And there was that wretched Guido Bartaldi behaving as if he owned the police station.'

'Well,' Violetta said with a tolerant shrug. 'He is a great man in this region. His family have been here since the *quattrocento*.' She lowered her voice. 'You realise, of course, who he is?'

'He's a marquis,' Clare said wearily. 'That was made more than clear.'

'Not just that.' Violetta spread her hands dramatically.

'Even you, *carissima*, who takes no interest in such things, must have heard of Bartaldi's, the great jewellers.'

'My God,' Clare said slowly. 'So that's why the name seemed familiar. It just never occurred to me...' She shook her head. 'Maybe I didn't expect to find an aristocrat running a jewellery business. Isn't it a little beneath him—that type of thing?'

'It is not merely a business, *cara*.' Violetta sounded shocked. 'With the Bartaldis, the working of gold and precious stones has become an art form. It all began in the sixteenth century.'

She shrugged again. 'There was a younger son—the black sheep, I suppose, of the family. He was sent into exile by his father, after a quarrel, and rather than starve he became apprenticed to one of the great goldsmiths of Siena. He had a flair for design, an eye for beauty and consummate taste, all of which he passed down to future generations. Eventually, he married his master's daughter, and bought his business.'

'And a shrewd eye for the main chance,' Clare said drily. 'He seems to have passed that on too.'

'And when the main branch of the family became weakened, and died out,' Violetta went on, 'his descendants took over the title and estates.'

'Now why does that not surprise me?' Clare muttered.

'And it is not just gold and jewellery now, you understand, although they remain one of the most prestigious companies in the world. Guido Bartaldi has recently diversified and opened a chain of boutiques selling the most exquisite leather goods, and scent to die for.' She sighed joyously. 'His "Tentazione" is quite heavenly.'

And naturally he'd have to call it 'Temptation', Clare thought sourly. Named for himself, no doubt.

She said drily, 'I imagine the price will be equally celestial. I remember now—I saw the shop in Rome when it first opened. The window display was one white satin chair, with a long black kid glove draped over it, and a red rose on the floor. The ladies who shop were treading on each other to get in there.'

'Hoping that Bartaldi would be there in person, no doubt.' Violetta's smile was cat-like. 'He is not exactly handsome, I think, but so attractive, like *il diavolo*. And still a bachelor.'

'But not for much longer.' Clare carefully selected another cake. 'He's going to marry his ward, poor little soul.'

'You pity her?' Violetta shook her head. 'Few women would agree, *mia cara*.'

Clare gave her a straight look. 'She doesn't want him, Violetta.'

'Then she is crazy.' Her godmother poured more coffee. 'It is one thing for a man to be successful and fabulously wealthy. *Per Dio*, one could almost say it was enough. But when he also has sex appeal—such formidable *attrazione del sesso*—then he is irresistible.' She winked. 'And the little Paola will not resist long, I think. Not when he has her in his bed.'

Clare found she was putting down her cake, not only uneaten, but suddenly unwanted.

She said, 'According to Paola, he has a mistress in Siena.'

'Which proves only that he is very much a man,' Violetta said comfortably. 'Do not be prim, *carissima*. It does not become you. And all will change when he marries—for a while at least,' she added with charming cynicism.

'But if so many other women want him,' Clare persisted. 'Why choose one who doesn't?'

'Who can say? Possibly because she is young and malleable, and comes from good breeding stock. No doubt he wishes for children. And the girl will be a *Marchesa*. It is a good bargain.'

'Well, it wouldn't suit me,' Clare said with sudden fierceness. She got to her feet. 'Darling, would you mind very much if I had a rest before dinner? I—I've got rather a headache. All the stress, I suppose.'

'Poor little one.' Violetta's sympathy was instant and genuine. 'And I have been bothering you with my chatter. Go and lie down, *mia cara*, and I will tell Angelina to bring you some of my special drops. Your headache will be gone in no time.'

Her headache, perhaps, Clare thought, as she went slowly up the curving marble staircase. But she was totally unsure what to do about the painful feeling of emptiness which had assailed her with incredible and inexplicable suddenness.

Except, she thought wearily, pretend, for all she was worth, that it didn't exist.

But it was not to be dismissed so easily. It was there, within her, like a great aching void.

And, as she lay on the bed, staring up at the ornately gilded ceiling fan revolving slowly above her, she was also unable to close her mind against the image of Guido Bartaldi's eyes burning into hers like a dark flame. Or the caress of his voice saying *'Chiara'*.

And that, she thought, was infinitely worse.

CHAPTER THREE

THE headache drops which Angelina had duly brought must have done the trick, because Clare found she had been able to sleep a little, and woke feeling calmer and more composed.

A long, scented soak in a warm tub helped restore her equilibrium still further. Afterwards there was the usual array of body lotion, eau de toilette, and scents in the personalised crystal flasks that Violetta favoured.

Clare uncapped the body lotion, sniffing it luxuriously, then smoothing it into her skin with sensuous pleasure, breathing in the aroma that the warmth of her body released.

Usually she chose very light fragrances, but this one was different—almost exotic with its rich, seductive tones of lily and jasmine. But a little sophistication might make her feel better, she thought.

As she dressed, Clare reviewed with satisfaction the hours ahead. Unless guests had been invited, the evenings invariably followed the same pattern.

First, she would join Violetta for an *aperitivo* on the rose terrace which gave the villa its name. Then they would indulge themselves with one of Angelina's long, delicious dinners. Afterwards, the lamps would be lit in the *salone*, and they would listen to music and chat while Violetta stitched her *petit point*.

She sighed happily, and skimmed through the clothes she'd brought with her. Her godmother enjoyed investing her evenings with certain formality, so she passed over her casual shirts and skirts, opting for one of her newer acquisitions, a simple ankle-length dress, with short sleeves and a vee neckline, in a silky crêpe fabric. Its deep ruby colour emphasised the paleness of her hair, and gave added warmth to the cream of her skin.

One of my better buys, she thought with satisfaction, taking a long and critical look at herself as she turned slowly in front of the full-length mirror.

She darkened her long lashes with mascara, and touched a dark rose colour to her mouth before she went down.

As she walked across the *salone* to the long glass doors which gave access to the terrace, she heard Violetta's charming throaty laughter.

Oh, Clare thought, checking slightly, so she has invited guests after all. She didn't tell me.

She found herself hoping it was the Arnoldinis, because that would mean cards instead of polite conversation after dinner, and she would not be expected to join in.

So I can let them get settled into the game, then plead tiredness and have an early night, she thought.

Smiling, she walked out on to the terrace, words of greeting already forming on her lips.

And checked again, because Violetta's guest, seated beside her on the cushioned seat in the shade of a big striped umbrella, was Guido Bartaldi.

He saw her at once, and, rising, made her a slight bow, the formality of the gesture slightly belied by the spark of amusement dancing in his dark eyes as he observed her shocked expression.

And what was she supposed to do in return? Clare wondered, rendered momentarily mute with outrage. Curtsy?

At last she found her voice. 'What are you doing here?' she demanded, dispensing with any preliminary niceties.

'Clare, *mia cara*,' Violetta intervened with a touch of reproach. 'The Marchese has called to make sure you completed your journey here in safety. So kind of him,' she added, bestowing one of her dazzling smiles on their visitor.

She was wearing mist-grey chiffon, with a discreet shimmer of diamonds at her throat and in her ears. And the Marchese seemed to have guessed her views on appropriate dress, because the casual clothes he'd been wearing earlier had been replaced by an elegant charcoal suit, set off by an impeccable white shirt and a silk tie in sombre jewel colours.

Violetta, Clare realised crossly, was looking at him as if she could eat him.

Not that she could wholly be blamed for that, she admitted, her mouth tightening. Earlier that day, even when she'd been scared almost witless, she had been able to recognise that, without even trying, he packed a formidable sexual punch.

And this evening, for whatever reason, he seemed to be trying...

'I have apologised to Signora Andreati for intruding in this way, but I had to set my mind at rest,' Guido Bartaldi said smoothly. 'You seemed—overwrought when we parted today.'

'Really?' Clare asked icily. 'I thought I was perfectly calm.'

'Yet your godmother has been telling me you retired with a headache. I hope you are fully recovered.'

'My head is fine,' she said shortly. *The pain now seems to be in my neck.*

'Ring the bell for Angelina, dearest,' Violetta said hastily. 'The Marchese and I are enjoying a Campari soda. I know that is your favourite too.'

Clare would have given a great deal to say tartly that she didn't want a drink, or any dinner, for that matter, and then withdraw in a marked manner. But that would only embarrass Violetta, who was clearly thrilled by her unexpected visitor, and Clare was far too fond of her to risk that.

And at that moment Angelina, all smiles, came bustling out with her Campari, and a plate of tiny *crostini* which she placed on the wrought-iron table in front of Violetta.

So, Clare would just have to make the best of things. Carefully she chose a chair on the other side of her godmother, deliberately interposing Violetta between herself and Guido Bartaldi, who resumed his own seat with a faint, infuriating smile.

He said, 'I also wished to assure you that your raincoat will be returned to you as soon as it has been cleaned.'

Clare gulped some Campari. 'Thank you.'

'It's nothing.' He paused. 'Paola was sorry not to be able to thank you in person for your care of her.'

'That doesn't matter.' Clare hesitated, unwilling to prolong the conversation, but not wanting to earn herself black marks from Violetta for being discourteous. She cleared her throat. 'How—how is she?'

He shrugged a shoulder. 'Not happy, but that is natural.'

'Entirely,' Clare said with emphasis.

'But she is young,' he went on, as if he hadn't heard. 'She will get over it. Indeed, I intend to make every effort to see that she does.'

'Lucky Paola.' Clare kept her voice expressionless and her eyes on her glass.

'I doubt she would agree with you,' he said softly. 'But I can appreciate that her social contacts locally are limited, especially when I am away on business so much. And, as I was explaining to the Signora, that is another reason for my visit. I hope you will both be our guests at dinner at the Villa Minerva tomorrow evening.'

'And I have told the Marchese that we would be delighted, *mia cara*. Is it not so?'

Clare put down her *crostini* untasted. No, she thought furiously, it was not so, and Guido Bartaldi knew perfectly well that she'd rather be boiled in oil than go to dinner at his rotten house. In fact, there wasn't enough space on the planet to separate them to her satisfaction.

I feel a subsequent engagement coming on, she thought grimly. Or at least a migraine. If not a brain tumour.

She fought to keep her voice level. 'Thank you. I— shall look forward to it.'

He said gently, 'You are too gracious,' and turned his attention back to Violetta, whom he treated with a charming deference bordering on flirtation. And she, of course, was lapping it up with roguish decorum.

Clare sat rigidly in her chair, clutching her glass as if it was her last hold on sanity—or safety.

Because she was suddenly frightened again. Because she didn't believe that he was motivated by any concern for her well-being, or remotely interested in restoring her raincoat to her. There was more to it than that.

Back in Barezzo, she'd experienced the power of this man. And she'd dared to antagonise him. The money he'd offered her was the merest drop in the ocean when compared with his total wealth. But that didn't mean he'd enjoyed seeing it torn in pieces and thrown at him.

It had seemed a grand gesture at the time. Now she was afraid she might live to regret it. Because he was not a man to shrug off that kind of affront—especially from a woman.

Something warned her that behind the smile and the silken elegance was steel. And beyond the steel lurked pure pagan.

She knew it as well as she knew her own reflection in a mirror. And she hoped she would only encounter the steel.

Angelina appeared in the terrace. 'The telephone for you, *signora*. It is Monsignor Caprani.'

'I will come.' Violetta rose to her feet, and Guido Bartaldi stood up too. 'No, no, Marchese, please stay. I shall not be long. And in the meantime Clare will be glad to entertain you.'

'Alas, I must get back.' His regret sounded almost genuine, Clare thought, seething. 'My uncle is expected from Venice some time this evening. But I shall look forward to welcoming yourself and the *signorina* to my own small world tomorrow. *Arrivederci*.' He took Violetta's hand and raised it to his lips. 'Until then.'

When she had fluttered back into the house, he turned and looked down at Clare, who stared back inimically.

'*Per Dio*.' His mouth twisted. 'I think if I was dining here tonight, I would ask to have my food tasted.'

She said huskily, 'What's going on? What do you want?'

'As to that,' he said slowly, 'I do not think I have quite made up my mind. But when I have, Chiara, be assured you will be the first to know. Now, wish me goodnight.'

Before she could resist, he reached down and pulled her up out of the chair and on to her feet in front of him, and only a few inches away.

He bent towards her, his gaze travelling from her frightened eyes to her parted lips.

She heard herself breathe, 'No.'

He laughed softly. With his free hand, he touched her cheek, running a questing thumb down the line of her throat, and she shivered and burned under his touch.

His fingers reached the neckline of her dress and hooked under it, urging the delicate fabric off her shoulder. Baring it. She felt his breath warm on her skin, then the brief, delicate brush of his lips along her collarbone.

He whispered, 'You are temptation itself, *mia bella*.'

Then she was free, and her dress was gently replaced. And before she could move or speak Guido Bartaldi had gone, walking away down the terrace steps into the twilit garden.

Clare stood, her arms wrapped around her body, her pulses shuddering uncontrollably. He had barely touched her. Her brain had registered that fiercely. But she felt, just the same, as if she'd been branded. That her flesh now bore some mark of his possession.

And this, she knew, was only the beginning.

In response to some hidden switch inside the house, the shaded lamps on the terrace came on, and instantly moths appeared, drawn by the lights and flinging themselves against them.

She thought, I know how they feel...

Violetta returned. 'Has the Marchese gone? Such a pity.' She sighed. 'If I were only twenty years younger. Sit down, *cara*, and Angelina will freshen our drinks.'

Clare sat, principally because her legs were shaking under her.

A thought occurred to her.

She said, 'Violetta, what's the scent that you put in my bathroom? The one I'm wearing?'

'But I was telling you about it, dear one. It's Bartaldi's own "Tentazione". Why?' Her godmother gave her a shrewd glance under her lashes. 'Did he recognise it?'

'Yes,' Clare said bitterly. 'Yes. I'm afraid he did.'

Dinner was not the relaxed, comfortable meal that Clare had anticipated after all.

For all her very real sophistication, Violetta was clearly thrilled to have received an invitation to the Villa Minerva, and eager to discuss it exhaustively.

'It is a very old house,' she said. 'Parts of it are said to date back to the time of the Etruscans, who, as you know, *cara*, fought the Romans for supremacy and lost.'

Pity, Clare thought, crumbling her bread. If they'd won the Bartaldis might never have seen the light of day.

'You've never visited there before?' she asked.

'No,' Violetta returned regretfully. 'But here at Cenacchio we are not exactly near neighbours to Veraggio. We move in our own circles.'

'Then it's a pity we agreed to go,' Clare argued. 'Particularly if it's a long way away.'

'The Marchese is aware of the inconvenience, and is sending a car for us.' Violetta sighed happily. 'He thinks of everything.'

She sent Clare a twinkling look. 'I think I have you to thank for this pleasant invitation, dear one.'

Clare bit her lip. 'I can't think why,' she said constrainedly.

'But naturally he wishes to make amends for all the confusion and unpleasantness of today.' Violetta nodded. 'He seems full of remorse for the hasty judgement he made.'

He's full of something, Clare thought broodingly. But I don't think it's repentance.

'Naturally, I have seen the Marchese at various social functions,' Violetta continued. 'But, as he says, he is not in the region very often. Perhaps when he marries, and has a family, that will change.'

She paused. 'Although his estates are excellently run in his absence, I understand. His manager, Antonio Lerucci, is said to be a charming young man, and most loyal and efficient.'

She chattered on, and Clare responded with interested noises and the occasional nod of her head, while trying to mentally detach herself.

She'd planned to stay at Cenacchio for at least two weeks. That might need revision now, she decided unhappily. She'd ring her agency tomorrow, and ask them to find her a job which would necessitate her urgent return to England.

And she would let a very long time elapse before she took another job in Italy, she decided broodingly. First she'd had Signor Dorelli to deal with, but, in retrospect, that had been no problem at all compared with Guido Bartaldi.

Dorelli had simply been a lecher and a fool. But the Marchese Bartaldi had a very different agenda. She knew it, although she couldn't even begin to make an educated guess at what it contained.

Every instinct, however, was shrieking at her to remove herself immediately from his sphere of influence.

I need to put the whole sorry mess behind me, and get on with my life, she thought. So I can't afford to stay.

'In the morning we will go into Perugia,' Violetta planned. 'And find a dress for you to wear. Something that will show you to your best advantage, *carissima*. It will be my birthday present to you.'

Clare was taken aback. 'I'm sure I have something that will do.'

Violetta tutted. 'When one is dealing with the Bartaldis, there is no question of making do. And you are too modest about your looks. We need something simple yet stunning.' She looked arch. 'The right setting for the jewel. Something the Marchese understands very well.'

'Violetta.' Clare was appalled. 'I don't know what you're thinking, but…'

Violetta shrugged. 'I think only that it would be good for you to be admired by an attractive man.' She paused. 'Has there been anyone since—what was his name?— James?'

'No,' Clare said quietly. 'Nor have I wanted there to be.'

'But that is so wrong,' her godmother protested. 'You are a warm and lovely girl. You cannot close yourself off from life because one fool preferred someone else.'

'I don't shut myself off,' Clare denied defensively. 'I have a job I like—friends—and I travel all over Europe. A lot of people locked into stale relationships would envy me.'

'I do not speak of those.' Violetta waved her hand. 'I speak of love, silly girl. Of overwhelming and complete love—like Dante felt for Beatrice, and Petrarch had for his Laura.'

Clare sighed. 'And Romeo for Juliet, I suppose, and we all know what happened to them.'

'Oh, when you are in this mood it is impossible to reason with you,' Violetta said huffily.

'That's certainly true if you're trying to pair me with the Marchese Bartaldi.' Clare tried to speak lightly, but she could feel the shoulder he'd kissed burning through the soft fabric of her dress.

Thank God Violetta didn't know about that, she thought ruefully.

She said. 'I'm sorry, darling, but the Marchese is the last man in the world I'd ever get involved with. Simply crossing his path has been more than enough, believe me. I've no wish to attract any more of his attention.'

She paused. 'Besides, you seem to forget that he's already chosen Paola,' she added carefully.

'Pah,' Violetta said. 'There has been no announcement. No formal engagement.' She gave a sigh of exasperation. 'In your shoes, cara, I would not hesitate.'

'A couple of hours ago, you seemed to think Paola would suit him ideally,' Clare said with asperity.

Violetta gave her a beatific smile. 'I had not met him then,' she said simply.

In spite of her tiredness, Clare found sleep frustratingly elusive that night. Her comfortable mattress seemed to have been stuffed with sand, and the big feather pillows moulded from concrete.

She tossed from one side of the big bed to the other, seeking a restful spot, while her mind turned endlessly, denying her any peace. And every thought that plagued her seemed to lead inexorably back to Guido Bartaldi.

Something else to thank him for, she thought peevishly, punching a pillow into submission.

Consequently, it was a wan, rather shadowy-eyed girl

who joined Violetta for a breakfast of cold meats, fresh fruit and coffee.

Not that she'd done anything to improve her appearance or disguise the ravages of her bad night. If the plan she'd formulated in the small hours was to work, she needed to look fairly deathly.

'Are you unwell, *cara*?' Her godmother, who'd been going through her morning mail, removed her reading glasses and gave her a concerned look. 'You are so pale.'

'I'll be fine,' said Clare, adding a brave smile for good measure.

'You have not forgotten we are going to Perugia this morning?'

'I'm looking forward to it,' said Clare, who had already decided that a refusal to go would only make Violetta suspicious. She would just have to make sure her godmother didn't spend too much on the promised dress, or choose something out of keeping with her usual lifestyle.

They parked at the Piazza degli Invalidi, and rode the escalators up to the Rocca Paolina. Clare always felt it was like rising up from the bowels of the earth, and she found the remains of the Rocca, with its low-vaulted roof and maze of dark passageways, many of them with water dripping down the walls, a disturbing place. Like being in an underground cave, she thought.

But this labyrinth of foundations was all the Perugians had left of the mighty Papal fortress intended to subdue their arrogance, and they'd even put up a plaque to commemorate its destruction three hundred years later.

Arrogance seemed to be a common trait among the Umbrian population—especially the men, Clare thought broodingly as they emerged into the sunlight of the Corso Vannucci.

And tonight she planned to dismantle a few stones from the fortress of self-assurance that the Marchese Bartaldi had built round himself.

Like many women for whom money is not an object, Violetta was an exacting shopper, and, after two hours had passed, Clare began to wonder if she intended to visit every boutique in the city. She herself had seen several dresses which would have been a welcome addition to her wardrobe, but Violetta had dismissed them.

'I know what I'm looking for,' she had declared, as she'd swept to the door. 'And that is not it.'

But eventually she said, 'Ah,' and nodded. 'Try this, *mia cara.*'

It was a slim, fluid full-length sheath in black silk jersey, long-sleeved with a deep square neck.

Too deep, Clare thought, viewing with dismay how much it revealed of her small rounded breasts. In fact, it moulded itself completely to her figure, clinging to her narrow waist and slender hips, and the skirt was slashed at one side to well above the knee.

'Violetta,' she protested. 'I can't wear this. It isn't— me. And what can I possibly wear underneath?'

But her words fell on deaf ears. Her godmother and the saleswoman merely exchanged speaking glances, and the dress was carried away to be reverently encased in tissue and placed in a carrying box.

By the time Violetta's credit card had financed high-heeled black kid sandals and a matching evening purse it was almost time for the shops to close for the long afternoon break.

'Most satisfactory,' Violetta declared with a cat-like smile. 'And now, *mia cara*, we will enjoy some lunch.'

But as they walked up the street, Clare was nudged

by her godmother. 'See—across the street? It is Bartaldi's. Let us look.'

Unwillingly, Clare found herself propelled across the street to the shop. The window display was as expensive and glamorous as she could have imagined—a blaze of exquisitely fashioned gold necklaces, pendants, bracelets and rings, as well as a tempting range of *etui* and other small, desirable *objets*. She felt as if she should close her eyes to avoid being dazzled.

'Beautiful, is it not?' Violetta breathed.

'Amazing,' Clare agreed levelly. 'If a bit overwhelming.'

Secretly, she preferred the adjoining window, which had a display of semi-precious stones. Her eyes strayed almost covetously from the glow of topaz to the mystery of aquamarine and the brilliance of jade and amethyst, again all set in gold.

'Many of the designs are drawn from the Etruscan,' Violetta explained, 'while others have a truly Renaissance spirit, don't you think? And they say Guido Bartaldi has been the guiding light behind it all. That he has the soul of a Renaissance prince.'

'Really?' Clare said in a hollow voice.

The soul of a *condottiere*, she thought smoulderingly. A robber baron.

She felt strange suddenly—uncomfortable—standing here outside these premises, staring at all this beauty that he'd had a hand in creating. As if she was intruding on something that was deeply personal to him.

It was time to act, she realised—in more ways than one.

She frowned unhappily. 'Violetta, I'm not very hungry. Would you mind if we missed lunch and went straight home? I—I'm feeling a little giddy.'

'Then we will not consider the escalators,' Violetta said immediately, snapping her fingers for a taxi to take them down the long hill to the car park.

Clare felt like a worm on the drive back to Cenacchio, aware of the anxious glances being directed at her, but that did not stop her from making a strangled request for the car to stop at one point.

And when they arrived back at the Villa Rosa, she whispered a strained apology, and made an immediate beeline for her room.

She undressed, put on a cotton wrap, and lay down on the bed, watching the sunlight play through the shutters.

I'm a wretch, she thought penitently, but it's in a good cause. Because there's no way I'm going to the Villa Minerva for dinner tonight.

In the end, she dozed a little, only to be rudely awoken by the unexpected arrival of Violetta's own doctor from Cenacchio.

Groaning inwardly, Clare submitted to having her pulse taken, her heart sounded, and her blood pressure checked.

'I think perhaps it's stress,' she ventured in response to his questions, and gave a condensed history of the past thirty-six hours. 'I had nightmares last night, and I can't stop thinking about those men with guns.' She shuddered and put her hands over her face.

The doctor made shocked noises, then prescribed rest, quiet, and a mild sedative. All of which Clare agreed to with outward meekness and inward jubilation.

'Such a terrible pity,' Violetta said mournfully, after the doctor's departure. 'I will phone the Villa Minerva, and tell the Marchese that we are unable to join him for dinner.'

Clare lifted herself on to an elbow. 'But there's no need for that,' she exclaimed. 'You can go, darling. And I'll just stay here quietly, as the doctor said.'

'But I cannot possibly leave you.' Her godmother was shocked. 'You are ill. I must take care of you, *cara*.'

'By sitting here watching me sleep? Because that's what I shall do once I've taken these tablets.' Clare shook her head. 'Violetta, that's just silly and I won't allow it.'

Violetta protested, but Clare gently but firmly overruled her.

'You know you're dying to see the house,' she said. 'And you can tell me all about it afterwards. Besides, you can give the Marchese my sincere regrets,' she added mendaciously.

'Well, if you are sure,' Violetta said reluctantly. 'And, of course, Angelina will be here to keep an eye on you.'

And watch me stage a lightning recovery as soon as the Marchese's car has departed, Clare thought with guilty relish.

When her godmother had gone to dress, Clare got off the bed and went and sat by the open window, watching the late-afternoon sunlight dance on the leaves of the flowering vine that grew up the side of her balcony.

She had a good view of the wide gravelled sweep in front of the house, and was able to see when the car from the Villa Minerva arrived, punctual to the minute.

What she did not expect was to see Guido Bartaldi emerge from the driving seat, casting an appraising glance at the façade of the house.

Hell's bells, Clare groaned to herself, shrinking back behind the shutter. He's come to fetch us himself. I hope he didn't see me.

She flew across the room and got into bed, pulling the

thin cover up to her chin, as if seeking some kind of sanctuary.

With luck Violetta, looking in to say goodnight, would think she was asleep, and leave her undisturbed.

But Fortune wasn't disposed to smile on her.

A few minutes later she heard a tap on her door, and Violetta saying softly, 'You have a visitor, *mia cara*.'

Clare wanted to shriek, *No*, but instead she kept her eyes closed, and her breathing soft and regular.

She heard footsteps approaching quietly.

'Ah,' Violetta whispered. 'The sedative the doctor left must have done its work.'

'So it would seem.'

Perhaps it was Clare's imagination working overtime, but she could have sworn there was a note of irony— even amusement—in Guido Bartaldi's deep drawl.

'Poor little one. She was so distressed to have to excuse herself tonight. She wanted so much to pay this visit.'

'I must make sure that there are other opportunities,' the hated voice said softly. 'You must let me know if she continues to feel ill. I have an interest in a good clinic near Assisi where she could be admitted for observation. As a precautionary measure, you understand. Now perhaps we should go, *signora*, and leave her in peace.'

Clare heard Violetta murmur her assent, and move away. A strand of hair was tickling her nose, and she wanted to brush it away, but something—some sixth sense—warned her to keep still.

Because Guido Bartaldi was still standing beside the bed, just waiting for her to betray the fact that she wasn't asleep at all.

She could feel the warmth of him, absorb the fragrance of his cologne. The knowledge of his presence made her skin tingle.

'A great actress has been lost to the stage, *mia bella*.' His low-voiced sardonic comment confirmed her worst suspicions. 'But I will not torment you any longer. Sleep well—and dream beautifully.'

To her fury, she felt his hand smooth away the annoying wisp of hair. Then his fingers took her chin, turning her head slightly on the pillow. And his mouth, briefly and sensuously, kissed her parted lips.

It took all the self-control she possessed to go on lying there, unmoving and unmoved, when she longed to leap up and slap him hard across that dark, mocking face. To call him all the names she could lay her tongue to.

Instead, eyes tight shut, she heard him walk away, and the bedroom door close behind him. Or had it? Maybe it was another trick.

It wasn't until she heard the sound of the car moving off down the drive that she dared relax her new rigidity and sit up.

There were tears of anger in her eyes, and she scrubbed fiercely at her mouth with the back of her hand, as a child might do.

'Tomorrow,' she vowed aloud, her voice shaking. 'Tomorrow I'm going home. And I'm making sure that I never—ever—have to set eyes on that bastard again.'

CHAPTER FOUR

VIOLETTA did not return home from the dinner party until well after midnight.

Clare, lying sleepless, saw the headlights of the car sweep across her ceiling and tensed, wondering if the Marchese had acted as chauffeur again, and whether she could expect another visit.

But, to her relief, she was left undisturbed, even by Violetta.

She'd spent a restless evening. In the end, sheer hunger had driven her downstairs, and Angelina, delighted to hear how much better she was feeling, had conjured up a thick bean soup followed by a creamy omelette served with tiny mushrooms and grilled baby tomatoes.

Clare had stretched out on one of the sofas in the *salone* and put on some music, but even this tried and tested procedure had not persuaded her to relax.

Her mind had been too full, and revolving almost exclusively around one subject—Guido Bartaldi.

It was infuriating to have to acknowledge the hold he'd taken on her imagination. His image seemed locked immutably into her brain, and she resented it.

She couldn't handle his constant and almost casual reappearance in her life. But she couldn't speak her mind about them for fear of upsetting Violetta, who was clearly happy to accept the Marchese at his own valuation.

But a man who was planning to marry, even if it was a marriage of convenience, should not be conducting a

56

flirtation with another girl, she argued, biting her lip. It was a despicable thing to do.

After James, she'd made a private vow to avoid any man who wasn't free to commit himself. And what a lot of them there seemed to be, she thought bitterly.

But with Guido Bartaldi it had already gone beyond simple flirtation—because he had touched—and kissed.

Her whole body shivered at the memory of his mouth on hers.

The worst part of it was her certainty that he knew exactly the effect that his caresses would evoke. It was a delicate, subtle form of torment, devised to punish her. To ensure she didn't embark on any more grand gestures to annoy him.

It was a stupid thing to do, she acknowledged sombrely. I should have seen that he was way out of my league as an adversary. Far better to have thanked him nicely, then stuffed the money in the poor box at the nearest church. Honour would have been satisfied on my part, and he'd have been none the wiser.

But it's too late for regrets. All I can do is cut my losses and go.

The shopping trip to Perugia had prevented her phoning the agency as she'd planned, but she'd do it first thing in the morning, she promised herself. And all she had to do then was find herself a flight back to Britain. Any class, any time, any airport, she added, pulling a face.

She felt tense, facing Violetta at the breakfast table the next morning, expecting a blow-by-blow account of everything that had been eaten, said and done at the Villa Minerva, but her godmother, surprisingly, said very little about it, apart from acknowledging that the house was

indeed beautiful, the food had been delicious, and that
she had enjoyed herself. After which she relapsed into
an unusually pensive state.

While, paradoxically, Clare found she was thirsting to
know more.

'What did you think of Paola?' she asked, in the end.

'Paola?' Violetta echoed. 'Ah, the young girl. She
seemed subdued. I think she was disappointed that you
were not there,' she added after a reflective pause. 'As,
indeed, were they all.'

She gave Clare a kind smile. 'Are you feeling more
yourself today, *mia cara*?'

'Oh, yes.' Clare flushed slightly. 'The medication the
doctor gave me seems to have worked miracles.' She
gave an awkward laugh. 'In fact, I'm fighting fit, and I
was thinking I really ought to get back to work again.'

'And I think you should enjoy your rest here with me,'
Violetta said firmly.

'There's nothing I'd like more,' Clare said quickly.
'But I haven't told the agency about the Dorelli fiasco
yet, and the chances are they'll want to reassign me
straight away. And I ought to contact Dad too.'

'But not for the next two weeks.' Violetta poured herself some more coffee. 'He is away, dearest. He has
taken *her*—' she invested the word with extraordinary
venom '—on a trip to San Francisco. He told me when
I telephoned him last week to ask for your address in
Rome, which I had mislaid.'

'Oh.' Clare digested this with dismay, then rallied.
'All the more reason for me to go back, then. I should
be there in case of an emergency with the business.'

Violetta shook her head. 'His assistant—Tricia, is it
not?—is doing that. So there is really nothing to take

you away,' she added dulcetly. 'Everything has worked for the best.'

'Yes,' Clare said too brightly, as she damned San Francisco, its bay, its hills, and its blameless citizens under her breath. 'Yes, of course.'

When breakfast was over, Violetta announced that she was driving into Cenacchio to the hairdresser.

'Do you wish to come with me, *mia cara*, or shall I ask Giacomo to place a lounger down by the pool for you?'

'That would be perfect,' Clare agreed. If she was forced to be on holiday, she thought, then she would behave like a holidaymaker.

When she went down to the pool below the rose terrace about an hour later, she found the lounger already in position, and Giacomo, Angelina's husband, who looked after the gardens at the villa, fussing with a sun umbrella. He was a small, wrinkled man with grey hair and black twinkling eyes, and he greeted Clare with his usual gap-toothed smile.

'Ah, *signorina*, each time you come here you are more like your dear mother, God give her rest.' He looked at her hands, clearly searching for rings, and tutted. 'But where is your husband? Where are the *bambini*?'

Clare laughed. 'I'm sorry to be such a disappointment, Giacomo, but we can't all be as lucky as Angelina.'

Giacomo shook his head reproachfully. 'Such a waste,' he told the sky, and went off, muttering to himself.

It was already bakingly hot, the sun dazzling on the water. It wasn't a very large pool, just big enough for Violetta to manage a few unhurried, decorous lengths as her token exercise for the day.

Clare found it cramped, but it looked inviting just the

same, she thought as she discarded her towelling wrap
and stretched out on the lounger in her simple black
bikini.

Now, she thought, shall I swim and then sunbathe, or
work on my tan for an hour, then cool off in the water?
Decisions, decisions.

And if that was all she had to trouble her, how happy
she would be. Only, it wasn't.

Because, try as she might, she couldn't convince herself that she'd seen the last of the Marchese Bartaldi.

He was there, all the time, at the back of her mind,
like a shadow in the sun.

And, more worryingly, he was physically present too,
at the Villa Minerva, within driving distance.

She picked up the bottle of high-factor sun lotion and
began to apply it to her arms and shoulders. Her skin
accepted the sun easily, turning a deep, smooth honey
colour without soreness, but she still treated the heat
with respect.

And she must do the same with Guido Bartaldi, she
thought, grimacing. Find some way to protect herself
against him. Or she could end up getting more badly
burned than she'd ever been in her life.

Dark glasses perched on her nose, she flicked through
some of Violetta's glossy magazines. It was like peeping
through a window into a different world, she thought,
smiling. A world where money was no object and your
life was designed for you, from the clothes you wore to
the glass you drank from. The kind of world where a
man like Guido Bartaldi reigned supreme.

For a minute, she let her mind dwell on that shop
window of jewellery, back in Perugia. There'd been one
gorgeous topaz pendant, glowing like a banked-down
fire in its heavy gold setting. She tried to imagine herself

walking into the shop, and pointing to it. Saying, I'll have that, without stopping to ask the price. Feeling the cool weight of the stone slipping down between her breasts...

Some chance, she thought, her mouth twisting with derision. She was one of the world's workers, and, though she earned a reasonable living, she'd always have to count the cost of anything she bought. And she wouldn't have it any other way, she added with a touch of defiance.

She felt restless again, the glamour and luxury depicted on the pages in front of her suddenly beginning to pall. Or was it that she was starting to feel a little bit envious?

Shaking her head in self-derision, she let the magazine drop to the ground and swung herself off the lounger. It was time for a swim, she decided, discarding her watch. Some hard physical exercise. Far healthier than crying for a moon she didn't even want.

The water felt wonderful, and she covered length after length with her strong, easy crawl. She was breathless when she pulled herself out on to the tiled edge, wringing the excess moisture out of her hair.

She towelled herself off, then adjusted the umbrella so that the lounger was completely shaded before she lay down again, turning on to her front and unfastening the clip of her bikini top.

Her bad night was catching up with her, she thought drowsily, pillowing her head on her folded arms and letting her body sink down into the soft cushions. The air felt very still, almost watchful, and the scent of the roses on the terrace above her was heavy—almost over-powering.

Almost as heavy as her own eyelids, Clare thought, and slept.

Something woke her eventually. She lay still for a moment, listening to the silence, wondering idly what had disturbed her. She turned her head slightly, and saw that a small wrought-iron table had been placed beside her, and on it a pitcher of iced fruit juice—peach, judging by its colour—and a glass.

Ah, she thought gratefully. Angelina. What a perfect way to be woken.

She sat up, pushing her disheveled hair back from her face, still slightly dazed from sleep, narrowing her eyes against the strength of the noonday sun as she reached for the pitcher.

And halted, hand outstretched, instinct telling her that the silence had changed in some way. That it contained another element.

Slowly, almost warily, she looked round, and felt the breath catch in her throat.

Guido Bartaldi was sitting about a couple of yards away from her, very much at ease in a cushioned chair. Long brown legs were revealed by brief navy shorts, and his bare feet were thrust into leather sandals, while a cream polo shirt set off tanned forearms and gave a glimpse of the shadowing of dark hair on his chest. His face was expressionless, his eyes hidden behind dark glasses as he surveyed her.

For a moment she was motionless, turned to stone, then she remembered just what he was seeing, and with a choking cry snatched up the towel from beside the lounger and huddled it protectively over her bare breasts.

'How the hell did you get in here?' Her voice rasped in shock. Embarrassed colour was flooding her face.

His brows lifted. 'I rang the bell at the entrance, and

was admitted like anyone else.' He pointed at the pitcher of juice. 'The housekeeper was about to bring you a cold drink, so I volunteered my services instead. Is there a problem?'

'Oh, none at all,' Clare said savagely. 'Tell me, does the phrase "Peeping Tom" mean anything to you?'

'Clearly not as much as it does to you,' he murmured.

Clare lifted her chin. 'Tell me something else, *signore*,' she invited dangerously. 'How much longer do you intend to maintain this—persecution?'

'I am sorry that you regard my visits in that light.' His own voice was deceptively mild. 'I am merely anxious to assure myself that you are fully restored to health.'

There were a number of succinct and very rude responses to that, Clare thought, smouldering. But uttering any of them would do her no lasting good.

Instead, 'I am well, as you see, *signore*,' she returned coolly. 'If that's all you wanted to know, I'd be glad to have my privacy restored.'

'No,' he said. 'That is not my sole reason for being here. In fact, I came to offer you a job.'

'A job?' she echoed in total disbelief. 'You want me to work for you?'

'Not directly.' He paused. 'I believe Paola told you she had an older woman as a companion?'

'Yes.' Clare's brows drew together. 'What of it?'

He said curtly, 'The signora is no longer part of my household. It was foolish to think that a woman of her age and outlook could reach any kind of rapport with a girl of Paola's temperament. She was not even a successful jailer.'

Clare realised that her towel was slipping and retrieved it hurriedly. She said, 'and that's what you're looking for? A better jailer?'

'No, no.' Guido Bartaldi made a dismissive gesture. 'That would be futile, even degrading. No, I want a companion for Paola that she can like and trust. Someone she can confide in.' He looked at her unsmilingly, and she wished she could see what was in his eyes. 'She talked to you. You seem the obvious choice.'

'I don't think so.' Clare shook her head vigorously. 'Apart from anything else, I'm a language teacher, not a chaperon.'

'That is all to the good. I have an international business. I travel extensively.' He paused. 'My wife will need to be fluent in other languages than her own.'

Clare tried to collect her flurried thoughts. 'You want me to teach Paola English?' She couldn't believe she was having this conversation. That he had the unadulterated nerve—the sheer arrogance—to make such a request of her.

'Together with some French.' He nodded, almost casually. 'I presume you are capable of this?'

She said between her teeth, 'Capable, yes. Willing, no.'

'I see. Have your recent experiences given you a distaste for Paola's company?'

'Paola,' she said, 'is not my main consideration.'

He said quietly, 'Then may I ask that she becomes so? She—needs you.'

Her lips parted in a gasp of astonishment. She said, 'Oh, this is ridiculous.'

'What is so laughable?'

'The entire situation.' She looked down at the towel she was clutching. 'And this in particular.'

She lay down again, gingerly tugging the towel from

beneath her and discarding it. She fitted her bikini top into place, and held it with one hand while she reached behind her back with the other to secure the little metal clip. But, however she struggled, it evaded her best efforts and remained determinedly undone.

'Allow me.' There was a ghost of laughter in his voice as he rose unhurriedly to his feet.

'I can manage,' she said with breathless haste, aware that she was blushing again.

Guido Bartaldi clicked his tongue reprovingly as he strolled to her side. 'You must learn not to fib, Chiara.'

Clare tensed uncontrollably as he bent over her, expecting to feel the brush of his fingers against her skin. Terrified at her own possible reaction.

But his fingers were brisk, almost clinical, as he dealt with the fastening, and stood up.

'Relax,' he advised. 'Your ordeal is at an end.'

'Thank you,' Clare said in a wooden voice, and he laughed openly as he returned to his chair.

'Do not strain civility too far, *mia bella*. You'd like to tell me to go to hell.'

She had to fight hard not to smile. 'That's the least of it, *signore*.'

'But, just the same,' he said. 'I would like you to consider my offer of employment.'

Clare looked back at him in silence, then swung herself off the lounger, picked up her wrap, slid her arms into the sleeves and tied the sash tightly round her waist, with ostentatious care.

'I think,' he said, 'that you are making some point.'

'How clever of you to notice.'

'It was not particularly difficult. Has anyone ever told you, Chiara, that subtlety is not your chief asset?' He crossed his legs. 'I infer you think you might find yourself in some kind of danger under my roof.'

'You're implying that I'm not?' She didn't disguise the scepticism in her voice, or in the look she sent him. 'You may not lack subtlety yourself, *signore*, but some of your behaviour towards me could be described as sexual harassment.'

'How clever of you to notice.' A smile played round the corners of his mouth. 'But you would have nothing further to fear on that score. Entering my household would act as an immediate safeguard. I am not in the habit of—harassing my employees.'

'That's reassuring,' she said. 'But I'm still not tempted.'

'You have not asked how much I would be prepared to pay to secure your services.'

'I don't want your money,' she said sharply.

'As you have already made clear,' he murmured.

'I mean I can't be bought.'

'And I am not looking for a slave.' His tone was equable. 'Or is that another reference to my wholesale corruption of public servants?'

Clare bit her lip. 'No.' She shook her head. 'But you see how it is, *signore*. There's no way that we could co-exist—you and I.' *And I—I couldn't take the risk,* she added silently.

'We would not have to co-exist,' he said shortly. 'I am hiring you to stay with Paola, not myself. My business interests cause me to be away a great deal. We would seldom meet.'

Clare sat down rather limply on the lounger. 'And how will Paola feel about that? She asked. 'It's hardly the ideal way to court your future wife.'

'Ah,' he said. 'You do not think that my absence will make her heart any fonder?'

She said bluntly, 'I'd say it would convince her that you don't give a damn about her.'

'Then she would be wrong.' He was unruffled. 'I care for her very deeply. But I am aware that she does not return my feelings. Or not yet.' He paused. 'I hope that you can, perhaps, change that.'

'I?' Clare echoed. 'How can I do that?'

'By bringing her to a more suitable frame of mind. By getting her to recognise that I can make her happy.'

Clare drew a deep breath. 'Let me understand this,' she demanded in outrage. 'You want me to turn a hostile, unruly girl into a submissive bride for you?'

He smiled at her. 'Exactly.'

There was a brief, fulminating silence, then she said shortly, 'It can't be done.'

'I think it altogether possible—if you try. Just bend that formidable will of yours to the problem, Chiara *mia*, and who knows what miracle might not ensue?'

'Perhaps it's not a problem I particularly wish to address.' Her mouth tightened. 'Just why do you want this marriage, *signore*?'

'I have a house,' he said. 'But it is not a home. I have a great name, but no heir. I have relationships, but not with a woman who can fill my heart to the exclusion of all others. Are those good enough reasons?'

Clare looked down her nose. 'It all sounds a little cold-blooded to me.'

'But you are so wrong,' he said softly. 'As my wife will discover for herself once her nights are spent in my arms.'

She looked down at the tiles at her feet, feeling the sudden startled colour flood her face. Aware of the urgent necessity to veil her eyes from him. Feeling some unfamiliar, confused emotion composed of envy and a kind of regret tremble inside her. And trying desperately to crush it down…

She said in a low voice, 'Maybe you should start convincing her of that now.'

'That would not be appropriate,' he told her coolly. 'We are not even officially engaged to each other.'

Back under control, she looked up, lifting her brows satirically. 'I did not think you were so conventional, Marchese.'

'But then you know so little about me, Chiara,' he came back at her, sardonically.

'That,' she said. 'Is my choice.' She rose to her feet again. 'I won't do as you ask. Because I can't understand why you'd want to marry anyone who's already run away from you once.'

He shrugged as he got out of his chair. 'Perhaps it is the nature of love—the girl to fly and the man to follow.' He paused. 'Is that your only reservation?'

'No.'

'Ah,' he said, and was silent for a moment. Then, 'Paola will be disappointed. It was her idea that you should take the Signora's place.'

'Please tell her I'm sorry.'

'I hope you will tell her yourself.' He paused again. 'And do not let your dislike for me prevent you from being her friend while you remain in Umbria. She would like very much for you to visit her.'

Clare swallowed 'I'm not sure that's such a good idea.'

'Why not?' Guido Bartaldi spread his hands enquiringly. 'I have accepted your decision. So, what harm can it do?'

Oh, God, thought Clare, you have no idea. And thank God you haven't...

Aloud, she said, 'I may not be around for much longer. After all, I have...' She paused swiftly, realising what she was about to say.

'A living to earn?' he supplied silkily, and accurately. 'And yet you will not take work when it is offered. How strange.'

'I'm a grown woman, *signore*. As I've said, I make my own choices.'

'A woman?' he queried thoughtfully. 'I wonder if it is true.'

'How—how dare you?' She glared at him, shock tightening her throat. 'My—personal circumstances are nothing to do with you.'

'*Basta*. I am not claiming that you are still physically a virgin,' he said impatiently. 'That is immaterial. What matters is that sometimes, when I look at you, Chiara, I see a frightened child hitting out at the world—and hurting only herself.'

She said icily, 'Thank you for the psychological profile. Remind me to do a run-down on you some time.' She paused. 'But tell Paola if she wants to visit me here, I'll be happy to see her. Maybe we can have a dolls' tea party.' She bent and picked up her towel and the magazines. 'Perhaps you'd excuse me now. I'm sure my godmother will be glad to see you before you go.'

'I think she is quite happy talking to my uncle.' He had the gall to sound amused. 'He was hoping to meet you, but I see you are not in the mood.

He walked over to her, and stood for a moment looking down at her.

'I have made you angry,' he said quietly. 'And also scared you a little, I think. I did not intend to.' He took her unresisting hand and raised it to his lips, swiftly and gently. '*Arrivederci*, Chiara.' His voice was low—intimate.

She felt the heat of the sun surrounding her like a golden web, closing her in with him as she stared at him mutely, caught in the thrall of the moment.

His tone changed—became brisk, almost businesslike. 'And if you should change your mind about the job I have offered, *naturalamente*, you have only to let me know.'

The pang of disappointment was so sharp she almost cried out.

Instead, she snatched her hand away, offering him a smile that glittered like a razor.

She said dulcetly, 'All hell will freeze over first, Marchese. Goodbye.'

And she walked away, her head held high, up the steps to the rose terrace, and into the house.

CHAPTER FIVE

CLARE made her way into the house by a side door, avoiding the *salone*.

She went straight to her room, where she stripped off her wrap and bikini and showered, revolving slowly under the warm cascade, tilting up her face, eyes closed, to its power, then cupping her hands and pouring water over her hair, and down her breasts and thighs until she felt cleansed and revived.

She towelled down slowly and thoroughly, discovering that she was watching her own reflection warily in the bathroom's long mirror, as if she might find some stranger she did not recognise looking back at her.

She put on clean underwear, then slipped into a pair of dark green silky culottes, and a matching sleeveless top with a scooped neckline.

As she was brushing her damp hair, she heard voices below her window, and, peeping out cautiously, saw Guido Bartaldi and an older man, tall, grey-haired and handsome, walking towards the chauffeured limousine awaiting them on the drive.

She sighed with relief, because she'd feared Violetta might have persuaded them to stay for lunch. And it would be useless to pretend ill health again.

She slid her feet into heel-less silver kid sandals, and went downstairs.

She found her godmother standing by the long glass doors leading on to the terrace, staring out at the garden, so deep in her reverie that she started when Clare spoke to her.

'Ah, *carissima*.' There was a note of reproach in her voice. 'I was wondering where you were. I wished to present you to the Conte did Mantelli.'

'I'm sorry.' Clare dropped a penitent kiss on her cheek. 'I got a little overheated in the garden, and went up to my room to cool off.' She looked round innocently. 'Have your visitors gone?'

'Yes.' Violetta gave her an old-fashioned look. 'But I do not flatter myself that they came to see me.' She paused. 'I understand the Marchese had a proposition for you.'

'Yes,' Clare said calmly. 'He wants me to act as chaperon for his bride-to-be.'

'That is what his uncle the Conte told me.' Violetta sighed. 'The girl Paola is a big problem to them all, I think. Clearly she needs someone *simpatico*, but with sense, to be her companion.' She shot Clare a sideways glance. 'I told the Conte you would be an ideal choice.'

'Does he know that forty-eight hours ago his nephew was trying to have me jailed?'

'Ah, but that was just a terrible misunderstanding,' Violetta protested. 'So unfortunate.'

'Unfortunate for me, certainly,' Clare agreed. 'I could have been deported. Unable to work here again.'

'But that has all changed now,' Violetta said coaxingly. 'And it would mean you would stay in Umbria, as I have always wished. It was always a sorrow to me that I had no children. And a daughter especially. This will allow me to see more of you while you earn a living.'

Clare bit her lip. 'I'm sorry, Violetta, but I turned the

Marchese down. I can't possibly work for him. You must see that.'

'I see nothing of the kind,' Violetta said with a touch of tartness. 'You would live in luxury, and be paid a generous salary simply to stop a tiresome girl from causing more trouble. How can you refuse?'

'Quite easily. It—it's not a cause to which I wish to devote a chunk of my life.' Clare studied the coral enamel on her toenails as if her life depended on it.

'But it would not even be for very long,' her godmother urged. 'The Conte tells me that he hopes Paola's wedding will take place at the earliest opportunity. Marriage, of course, will settle her.'

'So the Marchese Bartaldi intends,' Clare said evenly, feeling as if an icy fist had clenched inside her. 'In the meantime, it will do him no harm to act as her *simpatico* companion himself. Maybe he could start by giving up his mistress in Siena.' She sent Violetta a taut smile. 'I wonder what's for lunch? I'm starving.'

Over the next few days, Clare applied herself to enjoying her holiday with a kind of dogged determination. There was no further communication from the Villa Minerva, so it seemed that the Marchese had decided to accept his dismissal from her life.

Which is exactly what I want, Clare told herself robustly. And all I have to do now is put the whole sorry business out of my mind.

The weather was glorious, so part of each day was spent by the pool, where she swam and sunbathed, watched indulgently by Violetta, who sat rigorously safe-guarding her complexion with a parasol.

On one occasion they drove to Urbino, so that Clare

could see the art treasures in the magnificent Renaissance palace that towered over the city.

Another day they visited Assisi, where Violetta murmured sorrowfully over the damage caused by the earthquake to the two great basilicas of St Francis and Clare, which stood at opposite ends of the town, both of which were being rapidly restored, however, even down to the famous Giotto frescoes which had suffered so disastrously.

'Was it very frightening?' Clare asked.

Violetta shuddered. 'The whole earth seemed to rock, *mia cara*. But I was so lucky. A few tiles from the roof—some panes of glass—that was all. Elsewhere such hardship and tragedy.'

As they drove back to Cenacchio, Clare found herself looking up at the rugged Appennine hills which provided such a dramatic backdrop to the narrow road they were travelling on. They said wolves still lived on those steep, thickly forested slopes, and she could believe it. There was a wild, almost savage quality about them.

At the same time they looked so majestic—and eternal. As if nothing could move them. Yet the earth was such a fragile place, at the mercy of Nature in all kinds of ways, as the recent quakes had proved so drastically.

And even when the world seemed at peace, as it did today, there were other more personal storms to endure. Disturbed nights, with too vivid dreams, and, by day, a strange, aching emptiness that she could not escape, she thought, shivering.

'I need to stop in Cenacchio,' Violetta announced as they reached the small town. 'My attorney wishes me to sign some papers over the lease of a field. So tedious. Why don't you look at the shops, and we will meet at the *caffe* in the square in a half-hour, *cara*?'

Clare agreed readily to this plan, wandering happily round the narrow cobbled streets, window-shopping at the boutiques, pausing at a small bookshop to buy a local guide book, and, on impulse, a life of St Clare of Assisi.

At the delicatessen, she stared longingly at its mouth-watering displays of cheeses and sausages, and the enormous variety of goodies in jars and bottles.

Before she went home she would treat herself to some really good olive oil, she determined.

The half-hour was up, but there was no sign of Violetta at the *caffe*. Unperturbed, Clare seated herself at a table under the blue-striped awning, and ordered a cappuccino.

She began to glance through the life of the saint, finding to her amusement that her namesake was the patron of television.

Well, I suppose there has to be one, she thought, as she casually turned the pages.

When a shadow fell across the table, she assumed it was Violetta, and glanced up with a smile, only to find Paola gazing anxiously at her.

'Signorina—Clare?' Her face broke into an uncertain smile. 'I hoped it was you. Are you alone? May I join you?'

'Of course. I'm just waiting for my godmother.' Clare returned the smile politely but without any particular enthusiasm.

'Ah, the Signora Andreati. I was so pleased to meet her. *Si amabile. Si elegante.*'

'Yes, she's all of that,' Clare agreed, her tone softening, touched by the wistful note in Paola's voice.

The younger girl sat down beside Clare, and put a hand on her arm. 'I have so much wanted to see you. I wanted to say how sorry I was for all that Guido made you suffer.' She shook her head. '*Che bruto*. Did I not tell you?'

'Yes,' Clare acknowledged. 'But I don't think you should tell me again. Not when you're talking about the man you're going to marry.'

'*Niente paura,*' Paola asserted passionately. 'It will not happen.' She gave a wary look around her. 'But I need your help.'

Clare sighed. 'I'm sorry, Paola. But that wouldn't be very wise. And you don't really need help. You just have to say No and mean it.'

'You do not understand.' Paola lowered her voice to a whisper. 'His uncle is with us now, and they will force me to do as they say.'

Which pretty well confirmed what Violetta had told her, Clare thought, not without sympathy.

'Why not talk to the parish priest?' she suggested. 'I'm sure he isn't allowed to marry people against their will.'

'He does what Guido tells him,' Paola said sullenly. 'As they all do.'

Clare groaned inwardly. I don't need this, she thought. She said, 'Then the Marchese is hardly likely to take any notice of what I say either.'

'Oh, I do not mean that.' Paola's voice was conspiratorial. 'But if you came to live at the Villa Minerva, you could help me escape.'

'If memory serves, you tried that already,' Clare said drily. 'And if your *fidanzato* has all this power, he'd soon find you, like he did last time. Besides, where would you go?' She leaned back in her chair. 'Paola, the best thing you can do is try and talk Guido out of this marriage. Convince him that it would be a disaster.'

'Or, there is another way.' There was a glint of triumph in the other girl's eyes. 'I could always marry someone else.'

Clare felt her heart sink into her elegant sandals.

'You have someone in mind?' She tried to sound casual.

'You know I do.' Paola sounded shocked. 'It is Fabio, of course.'

'Naturalamente,' Clare said in a hollow voice. 'I didn't realise he was back in the picture.'

'He made contact again through Carlotta.' Paola lowered her voice mysteriously. 'Guido accused him of wanting only my fortune—said terrible, threatening things to him. For a while, he was frightened, but now he knows he cannot live without me, and he will risk anything.'

I bet, Clare thought stonily, tempted to take Paola by her pretty shoulders and shake her until her teeth rattled.

But that would solve nothing. In fact, it would probably harden Paola's determination to ruin her life. And Clare hadn't the slightest doubt that would be the outcome if the silly girl wasn't stopped.

She could, of course, dump the whole thing on Guido Bartaldi, but he would probably try and put a stop to the affair by locking Paola in a convent, or something equally mediaeval. And that would simply turn her into a martyr, and make her more stubborn than ever.

No, Paola must somehow be made to see Fabio for what he really was. To be disillusioned so deeply that he would never stand a cat in hell's chance with her again. Nor anyone else of his ilk, she added grimly.

But if Paola eluded Fabio's frying pan, she should not be despatched to the Marchese's fire either.

They're just so wrong for each other, Clare told herself vehemently. It would be a wretched marriage for both of them.

Although there was no reason why she should care what kind of a mess Guido Bartaldi created for himself, she admitted, biting her lip.

No, Paola was her concern here. She might be young and giddy, but she didn't deserve either of the fates that were being wished on her.

But, Clare conceded, she needed to learn to grow up, and stand on her own two feet. Become her own rescuer, instead of relying on other people.

I wonder if she's capable of that? Clare thought, stealing a sideways glance at the lovely face with its full, sulky mouth. So far, she's spent most of her time being handed round like a parcel, and letting men dictate to her. I wonder if I could show her that there's more to life than that?

'Clare—you do not speak.' Paola's voice was petulant. 'What are you thinking?'

Clare smiled at her calmly. 'I'm just trying to decide what the best plan of action might be.'

'Then you will help me?' The younger girl's face was suddenly transfigured. 'But how? Guido told me he asked you to take the place of the Signora, but you would not. And it will be hard for us to keep in touch when you are in Cenacchio. I cannot always think of reasons to come here.'

'Then I'll just have to come to the Villa Minerva,' Clare said resignedly.

'You mean it? You will tell Guido you have changed your mind? Oh, that is wonderful.'

'Yes,' Clare said, wincing inwardly. 'I'll tell him.'

And, as if she'd conjured him up from some dark place in her soul, she saw him walking across the square towards them, with Violetta chatting vivaciously at his side.

'Guido,' Paola carolled. 'Guess what. Clare says she will be my companion after all. Isn't that good news?'

Guido halted, his brows lifting as his dark gaze swept from Paola's triumphant face to Clare's tense figure.

'I am overwhelmed,' he said courteously, after a pause. 'Particularly as you seemed so adamant at our last meeting. May I know what has brought about this change of heart?'

'I've had time to think things over,' Clare returned evenly. 'And I realise there could be mutual advantages in the situation. I planned to spend a few months in Italy, and working locally I can continue to see Signora Andreati in my free time.'

She paused. 'I presume I shall have free time?' she added. 'That you won't expect me to maintain a round-the-clock watch on Paola?'

He gave her a long, dispassionate look. 'These are details, *signorina*. I am sure we can work out an arrangement that will be agreeable to us both.'

'Oh, not *signorina*,' Paola protested. 'So dull—so *antiquato*. You must say Clare, as I do. And she must call you Guido.'

'As I'm going to be the Marchese's employee, maybe a certain formality should be maintained.' Clare returned his cool look with compound interest.

'It shall be exactly as you wish—Miss Marriot. And staying in touch with your godmother should not be a problem either, as I hope very much she will consent to be my guest at the Villa Minerva for a few weeks. While you are—finding your feet, shall we say?' He turned the charm of his smile on Violetta. 'Well, *signora*, will you do us all the honour of accompanying the *signorina* when she joins my household?'

No way, thought Clare. No one's ever managed to winkle Violetta out of the Villa Rosa at this time of year. And just as well, because I'm going to need somewhere to retreat to. And Paola might need a temporary refuge too.

But, 'How very good of you. I should be delighted, Marchese,' Violetta proclaimed sweetly, offering him a melting look as he bowed over her hand.

'Naturally I do not wish to interfere with any plans you have made for her entertainment,' Guido continued. 'But it would be helpful if Miss Marriot could take up her duties as soon as possible.'

'That will be no problem,' Violetta assured him serenely. 'We are at your disposal, *signore*. Clare, indeed could join you tomorrow, and I will follow as soon as I have made the necessary arrangements at home.'

Clare found she was sitting with her mouth open, and closed it indignantly.

'Arrange my life, why don't you' she muttered under her breath.

She had the feeling that she was being swept along on some inexorable tide. That things were already out of her control. And it was not a sensation she relished.

She'd allowed her concern for Paola to railroad her into a decision she would certainly regret, she realised with resignation. But it wasn't irrevocable. She was no longer Guido Bartaldi's prisoner, and could leave whenever she wanted.

She came out of her less than reassuring reverie to the awareness that he was watching her, a faint smile slanting the corners of his mouth, as if his thoughts were providing him with some kind of private satisfaction.

She lifted her chin in silent challenge, wishing she could read his gaze. He wasn't wearing sunglasses today, so there was no artificial barrier between them, but it made no real difference. He was still an enigma to her. A puzzle she had no hope of solving.

But maybe that was a good thing, she told herself soberly. Arm's length, and more, was the safest distance with a man like him. She had already glimpsed what devastation even a fleeting intimacy with him could evoke. Just the memory of his hand—his mouth—on her skin made her tremble inside.

She could not afford any more such moments of weakness.

'Come, Paola.' Guido Bartaldi extended his hand. 'We should return home and prepare to receive our guests.'

The other girl pouted, but she rose readily enough and went to his side, sliding her arm through his with a casual familiarity that seemed to belie her earlier protests about their relationship.

Perhaps I won't have to do a thing, after all, Clare thought with an odd pang. Maybe all he needs is to court her properly—gently and romantically—and she'll forget all that other nonsense and fall into his hand like a piece of ripe fruit.

And that would solve a whole lot of problems, she thought, stifling a little sigh, as polite goodbyes were said and the Marchese and his future bride moved away across the square.

So why did she feel no happier at the prospect?

'You will need clothes,' Violetta planned, over more cappuccinos.

'I think we've been here before.' Clare gave her a

despairing look. 'I have a perfectly adequate wardrobe already.'

'Not for the Villa Minerva,' Violetta said firmly.

'For my position there,' Clare said steadily. 'You may be a guest, but I'm simply the hired help.'

'Why do you speak of yourself in such a way? You are going to be the little Paola's companion. You will be expected to join in her social life, so—you must dress appropriately.'

'I don't go around in rags now,' Clare said with spirit. 'And you've already paid for an evening dress for me. I don't need anything else.'

Violetta expelled a sigh of pure exasperation. '*Dio*, how can you be so stubborn—and so blind?' she demanded. 'Don't you see what an opportunity this is for you?'

'It's just another job, with, hopefully, a decent reference at the end of it,' Clare said calmly.

'But in the course of this job you will get to meet many people.' Violetta made a dramatic gesture that nearly sent her cappuccino flying. 'It could change your life.'

Clare gave her a level look. 'The people in question being men?' she suggested.

'Well?' Violetta said defensively. 'Is it so impossible? You are a beautiful girl. You do not seem to appreciate that.'

'Perhaps because I know how little it means.' Clare tried to speak lightly. 'James used to tell me I was the loveliest thing he'd ever seen. But I couldn't compete with Ginny Parrish trailing her father's millions past him.' Her smile was crooked. 'I suddenly found I was being lovely all by myself.'

'So that is what happened.' There was compassion in Violetta's bright eyes. 'You never spoke about it before.'

'I don't know why I'm talking about it now,' Clare said a touch wearily. 'Unless it's because I'm watching another merger masquerading as marriage, and it tends to revive unhappy memories.'

'*Cara*, not all men are like this—James. One day you will meet someone who will value you for yourself. Who will not care how much money you have.'

'I hope so.' Clare sighed. 'But I guarantee I won't be meeting him at the Villa Minerva. Because that isn't how it works.' She paused. 'Maybe we should be getting back. I need to pack my rags,' she added, deadpan.

'Oh, you are an impossible girl,' Violetta told her crossly.

'You're quite tricky yourself,' Clare countered. 'What on earth made you accept Guido Bartaldi's invitation? You never go anywhere in the summer.'

Violetta shrugged. 'He is not an easy man to refuse— as you have discovered, *carissima*,' she said airily. 'And it means we shall not be separated—which is kind of him.'

'Oh, he's a regular Good Samaritan,' Clare agreed with irony. 'And, of course, you'll be meeting—people too.' She gave a swift gurgle of laughter. 'Who knows? Maybe your life will be the one to change.'

'Now you are being ridiculous,' Violetta said with unwonted coolness. 'You know quite well that I shall never consider another relationship.'

'So you've always said.' Clare was taken aback. 'But surely you can't rule out the possibility.'

'I can and I will.' Violetta was looking positively ruffled. 'And I find I do not care for this foolish conversation.' She picked up her bag. 'If you are ready, let us go. And do not forget,' she threw over her shoulder, 'you were the first to change her mind.'

Clare followed her meekly to the car, bewildered by this sudden display of asperity.

It must be the Villa Minerva, she thought. The place has some kind of disruptive, discordant influence on everyone. And tomorrow I'll be there. So what effect will it have on me?

And she found a sudden warning shiver tingling down her spine.

CHAPTER SIX

CLARE woke with a sudden start, and lay for a moment, staring towards the shuttered window, wondering what had disturbed her.

On the last occasion that she'd been startled out of sleep it had, of course, been the doing of Guido Bartaldi.

She was almost afraid to turn her head and look round the room, in case she saw the shadow of his tall figure standing in some corner watching her.

Now you're just being paranoid, she told herself derisively.

Because there was no sound in the room other than birdsong, and nothing to see either, except the slatted pattern of sunlight falling across the floor.

Clare sighed, then took her watch from the night-table and studied it. It was still very early. No one in the house would be stirring yet, and there was no good reason for her to do so either. Except this vague feeling of disquiet assailing her.

And it was also too late for further sleep, she decided, drawing up her knees and resting her chin on them. Although she was still tired after another restless, dream-ridden night.

What is the matter with me? She asked herself angrily. I've always been the soundest of sleepers. And, if I had dreams, I didn't remember them particularly. And I certainly didn't carry them, like lumber, into the next day.

But here they were, buzzing around her head still, refusing to be dismissed or forgotten.

To her irritation, James had been there, of course, his smile charming her, his voice soft and cajoling as he tried to persuade her that the mere fact of his marriage to someone else did not have to interfere with their own relationship.

And she'd sat, watching him in disbelief as he sketched out the half-life he had planned for her future. Watching him retreating backwards down some long tunnel of her imagination, getting smaller with every step until he'd finally vanished.

The memory of it still had the power to make her shiver.

In reality, of course, they'd had a furious row, and he'd stormed out telling her brutally that she was middle class and small-minded, and that he'd come back when she was prepared to be an adult.

'Don't you mean an adulterer?' she'd yelled after him, anger keeping the tears of hurt and shock at bay.

But in the dream she'd been unable to speak or move. Only feel the pain of betrayal twisting in her like a knife. The horror of knowing that James, whom she loved—whom she'd believed had loved her—was perfectly ready to sacrifice her and everything they'd had together. To relegate her to some corner of his existence while Ginny's money bought her the status of wife.

'Of course, I don't love her like I love you,' he'd told her over and over again. 'You know that, darling. But it's always been understood we'd marry each other. Fixed up by the families years ago. Her father and mine do a lot of business together, you see. I—I can't afford to pull out. But it needn't make any difference—to us.'

And she'd replied, as she always had, 'It makes all the difference in the world, James. Because I can't afford to stay.'

In last night's dream she'd seen James again, standing at the altar in a great Gothic church, with Ginny beside him in her white dress and veil. And she'd tried to reach him—to run up the aisle and prevent the ceremony. To tell him he was making a terrible mistake.

But her legs and feet had felt like lead, and the harder she'd tried, the greater the distance had seemed to become between them.

And when, eventually, she'd got to his side and seized his arm, forcing him to turn and face her, it hadn't been James at all who'd stood looking down at her with smiling contempt, but Guido Bartaldi, his eyes like flint.

She could explain it all away, of course. The memories of James she'd thought were dead and buried had been revived by her conversation with Violetta. And as for the Marchese—well, he was never far from her thoughts, although it made her cringe to admit it, even to herself.

He was there, in her mind, she thought restively, as if he'd been etched there, impossible to erase.

But it wasn't really impossible. Time and distance would make him fade into obscurity, and set her free again.

She needed to be rid of him while it was still possible. Before he hurt her—damaged her beyond repair.

And taking herself off to live under his roof was quite the worst thing she could do.

I should never have agreed, she told herself, swallowing past the sudden tightness in her throat. It was crazy.

Because he was another James—the kind of man she most despised. A man marrying for convenience rather than any involvement of the heart. Someone prepared to treat his marriage as a licence to do anything he wanted.

And expecting herself, of all people, to reconcile his

intended bride to this unenviable fate, she thought furiously. Although he couldn't know, of course, what an insult this was. The kind of devastating memories it had evoked for her.

But it wasn't an insult she necessarily had to put up with...

The thought strayed idly into her mind, then took firmer hold, making her sit bolt upright, her mouth set with sudden determination.

'I don't have to do this,' she said aloud 'and I won't. I'm going to cut my losses and get out of here. Back to sanity. Back to safety.'

Although she didn't want to examine too closely the exact nature of the danger she was in, or its current depth.

She pushed back the sheet, and swung her legs to the floor.

She could leave right now, before anyone was any the wiser, she told herself. If she was quick—and quiet—she could be miles away before she was even missed. Her packing, after all, was done. All she needed was to put her bags in the rented Fiat—and drive.

And Violetta was unlikely to disturb her for several hours. Not when Clare had left her the previous evening with the excuse that she needed an early night to prepare her for the coming ordeal.

'Such an ordeal.' Violetta had cast her eyes to heaven. 'Most girls would give anything to take your place.'

'But I'm not most girls,' Clare had returned, kissing her cheek.

She'd been relieved to find that Violetta's sudden spurt of ill-temper had been short-lived, and that her godmother had soon reverted to her usual charming self once they were back at the Villa Rosa.

But I still don't fully understand what was going on, she admitted frowningly, as she grabbed some undies and a plain cream skirt and top and headed for the bathroom.

But Violetta's vagaries had to take second place in the scheme of things, as Clare showered and dressed and made her plans.

Returning to Rome was probably her safest bet, she thought, grimacing. It would be easier to stay hidden in a crowd—always supposing anyone was to come looking for her...

There she'd find a travel agent, and buy herself any ticket on any flight back to the UK.

She would leave a note for her godmother, saying simply that she'd changed her mind, and gone away to avoid embarrassment. She only hoped Violetta's invitation to the Villa Minerva would still stand in her absence, as she was clearly looking forward to it with keen anticipation.

After all, it's not her fault that I'm reneging on our bargain, she thought defensively. Although Guido Bartaldi might not see it that way. He would not be pleased to find his arrangements for Paola jettisoned like this.

But—in every war there were bound to be casualties. And she regarded her dealings with Guido Bartaldi as war-like in the extreme.

But the problem of Paola remained, of course, she admitted, biting her lip. Especially now that Fabio was around again to muddy the waters.

Paola was still little more than a child, after all. She didn't deserve to be left to the tender mercies of a man who was marrying her for commercial reasons—whether he was a confidence trickster, or a member of the Italian nobility, she added with a certain violence.

No, she didn't like the idea of leaving the girl in the lurch, but what choice did she have? Her own peace of mind had to be her priority.

I'll write to Violetta, she promised herself guiltily. Warn her about Fabio. She's been targeted by men like him ever since she was widowed, and she's seen them all off. She must be able to find some way of bringing Paola to her senses.

As she made her way quietly down the stairs, she could hear faint clattering from the kitchen regions, signalling that Angelina had started her day.

She opened the heavy wooden door with exaggerated care, wincing as the hinges creaked, and edged round it into the bright morning sunlight.

For a moment she was dazzled, and blinked. When she could see again, she realised there was a car parked at the foot of the steps—something long, dark and sporting.

And leaning against its bonnet was someone tall, dark and definitely unsporting.

Guido Bartaldi, totally at his ease, and looking as if he had all the time in the world.

Shock and disbelief turned her to stone. She stood, staring down at him, lips parted in silent horror.

'*Buongiorno.*' He looked up at her, and smiled, and she felt her heart turn over. 'It's a beautiful day.'

She found her voice. It emerged with something of a croak. 'What—what are you doing here?'

'I came to meet you—to escort you to the Villa Minerva.' He paused, his brows slanting mockingly as he focused on her travel bag. 'Something told me that you would wish to make an early start—and I see I was right.' He walked up the steps and took the bag from her unresisting hand. 'How good to know we are in such accord. It bodes well for the future, don't you think?'

'No, I don't.' Clare drew a deep breath. 'It was—considerate of you to think of me, but I'm quite capable of making my own way to your house.'

'I never doubted your capability, *mia cara*,' he tossed back over his shoulder. 'Merely your willingness to comply with our bargain. But perhaps I have a naturally suspicious mind.'

He put her bag in his boot, then walked round and opened the passenger door. 'Shall we go?'

Clare lifted a defiant chin. 'I have my own car, thank you.'

'Ah,' he said softly. 'The rented Fiat. It is no longer here.'

Clare swung round and found the parking place next to Violetta's car was indeed empty.

'Where is it?' she demanded.

His voice was silk. 'I arranged to have it collected earlier today, and returned to the hire company's office in Perugia. And also for the bill to be settled on your behalf. I hope this is agreeable to you.'

'It's far from agreeable,' Clare said fierily. 'How dare you make such arrangements without consulting me?'

'It is not easy to consult you,' he said, 'when you insist on being so determinedly asleep so much of the time.' He paused. 'Your godmother thought it was a good idea, when I spoke to her last night, and was happy to hand over the documentation and the keys.'

'Quite a little conspiracy,' Clare said icily. She realised now what had woken her. The sound of the Fiat being removed. 'I wasn't aware that hire companies started their activities at dawn.'

'They don't. But my associates do, when necessary.'
He let her digest this, then went on smoothly, 'Now,
shall we drop the subject, or continue this argument on
the journey? The choice is yours.'

'Really?' Clare queried bitterly. 'It seems to me that
all my choices have been pre-empted.'

He laughed. 'Not all of them, *cara*. Just those that
would not be to your advantage—or mine.'

Clare stood her ground. 'I haven't said goodbye to my
godmother yet.'

'I did not realise you had planned to,' he murmured,
his mouth twisting. 'As it is, she asked last night not to
be disturbed, and said she would see you very soon.'
The dark eyes met hers. Held them. 'Is there another
problem, or may we begin our drive?'

Now, if ever, was the moment to tell him she'd
changed her mind. That she had no intention of going
anywhere with him. This was her chance to go back into
the house, shut herself into her room, and tell Angelina
that she did not wish to meet the Marchese Bartaldi
again while she was under Violetta's roof.

But the words wouldn't come. Not when he was—
looking at her. Making her look back at him.

Making her realise that there was no escape. Because
Fate had intervened, and the die had been cast for her.

She thought, with a kind of frantic calm, It's too late.
It's all far too late—and—somehow—it always has
been.

And walked slowly down the steps to the waiting car.

'You are very quiet.'

Clare, who'd been sitting, staring rigidly through the
windscreen, her hands gripped together in her lap for the

first fifteen minutes of the journey, started slightly as Guido spoke.

'I think "stunned" would be a more apposite word,' she returned constrainedly.

'Are you a nervous passenger? Am I going too fast for you?'

Now there, thought Clare, was a loaded question.

Aloud she said, coolly, 'I'm not nervous. As I'm sure you already know, Marchese, you're a very good driver.'

The road they were taking twisted and twined between tall, heavily forested hills, but she'd been aware from the first that the car's power was being tightly, even ruthlessly controlled.

As he controls everything else, she thought tautly.

And she was deeply conscious, too, of Guido Bartaldi's own physical proximity to her in the comparatively confined conditions of the vehicle. Watching his hand change gear only inches from her thigh. The play of muscle in his forearms as he turned the wheel.

Each slight action or reaction made its own individual impact on her senses.

It was an effort to breathe normally, she realised, swallowing. To ignore the heightened pulsing of her bloodstream. Her whole body's tense response to his nearness.

He shot a glance at her. 'Then perhaps you're sulking because I whisked you away with me.'

She gasped indignantly. 'I don't sulk. But are you quite so high-handed with all your staff?'

'I don't know.' There was a note of amusement in his voice. 'And I am also the wrong person to ask. Maybe you should consult them.'

He paused. 'But I should make one thing clear, Chiara. I do not regard you simply as a member of staff.'

She stiffened. Her swift sideways glance was wary. 'I don't understand. You asked me to work for you. That was the deal.'

'*Si,*' he agreed. 'But I would much prefer you to work with me—as a colleague. Even a friend.'

Pain lanced through her. 'That—can't happen.'

'Why not? After all, while you live under my roof, *cara mia*, you will be almost a member of the family.'

'You're paying me a salary, *signore*. In my book that makes me an employee—and I wouldn't have it any other way,' she added with emphasis, then hesitated. 'And while we're discussing preferences, I'd rather you didn't use—endearments when you speak to me. I feel it's—inappropriate.'

There was a silence, then, 'So what do you wish to be called?'

She bit her lip. 'I—I don't know. How did you address Paola's previous companion?'

'As "*signora*",' he said gravely.

'Then maybe we should be equally formal.'

'The two cases are hardly the same. The Signora was a much older woman. And she did not have hair like sunlight and a honey mouth. You see the difficulty?'

'If you persist with remarks like that, *signore*,' Clare said coldly, 'working for you will not just be difficult— but impossible. Maybe you should stop the car right here and now.'

'*Per Dio,*' he said. 'So I am forbidden even the mildest flirtation?'

'By no means,' Clare returned primly, furiously aware that he was laughing at her. 'Just as long as it's directed at Paola.'

'How dull,' he murmured.

Clare swallowed. 'If that's how you feel, maybe you

should think again about being married. It seems to me that you're heading for disaster.'

'And it seems to me,' he said, 'that you are very candid—for an employee.' He allowed the point to register, then continued smoothly. 'But put your mind at rest. I promise I am becoming more reconciled to my fate with every day that passes.'

'But yours isn't the only point of view that counts. Can you honestly say the same for Paola?'

He shrugged. 'That is for you to find out.'

'And if I can't do what you want?' she said slowly. 'If she won't accept this marriage—what then?'

He laughed. 'I have infinite faith in your powers of persuasion, *mia bella*. Besides,' he added, his voice hardening slightly, 'you must see that Paola needs to be married. There are no other options open to her. She is not trained for a career, although she has spoken vaguely of modelling, and she has no qualifications. At school, she was regarded as a charming feather-brain.'

'Maybe she'd be very good at modeling,' Clare suggested, without much hope.

'She has the looks,' he agreed. 'But no discipline. A life that required her to get out of bed before midday would have little appeal. I doubt she has the stamina either. It is a physically taxing existence.'

Clare bit her lip. 'Poor Paola.'

He shook his head. 'You need not pity her. Because she will be happy—and safe. She needs above all someone who will look after her, and prevent her from doing something reckless and ruinous.'

'Like marrying the wrong man,' Clare said bitterly.

He slanted a smile at her. 'But by the time the wedding takes place, *mia bella*, she will not think that. I guarantee it.'

A curious emotion stirred inside Clare, compounded of anger and something perilously like envy.

She said, 'Heaven help her.'

'Heaven is where the best marriages are made, Chiara.' The undercurrent of laughter in his voice goaded her. 'Isn't that what they say?'

'I think,' Clare said coldly, 'that "they" talk an awful lot of nonsense.' And relapsed into a fulminating silence.

The Villa Minerva lay at the head of a small valley, a tawny sprawl of a house, crowned in faded terracotta tiles and enclosed protectively by the encircling arms of the craggy dark green slopes which reared behind it.

Like an old, proud lion sleeping in the sun, Clare thought with an involuntary lift of her heart, as she caught her first glimpse of it through the trees that lined its steep, private road.

She'd expected something far more stately and grand, even intimidating. But, apart from its considerable size, the villa looked reassuringly home-like.

She thought, 'It's beautiful,' and only realised she'd spoken aloud when she caught the flicker of her companion's smile, and a murmured *'Grazie.'*

Minutes later, the car negotiated a gateway guarded by tall stone pillars, and drove into a large paved court-yard fronting the house, where a fountain in the Baroque style sent lazy arcs of water curving into the sparkling air.

Guido had barely stopped the car at the foot of the short flight of steps which led up to a massively timbered front entrance, when Paola came running out to meet them.

'Clare, you have come.' Face and voice were stormy. 'I did not think it would happen—not when Guido has set his other jailer on me,' she added, giving the Marchese a venomous look as he emerged from the car.

'Ah,' he said. 'Then Tonio is here. *Bene.*'

'It is not good—' Paola began rebelliously, but Clare stepped in.

'Pardon me,' she said levelly, 'But I understood I was coming here as your companion, Paola. As a friend. Not a jailer. But if that's how you see me, I'll leave now.'

'No, I did not mean it.' Paola put a placatory hand on her sleeve. 'I spoke hastily. I was just so angry when Tonio arrived.'

'I cannot think why,' Guido said coldly. 'He is here on estate business to consult with me, and it is more convenient for him to stay in this house. His presence should not affect you. You need not even speak to him.'

'Not speak to him?' Paola's voice lifted in outrage. 'Someone I have known my entire life? Of course I shall talk to him.' She grabbed Clare's hand. 'Now come and see your room.'

'My luggage,' Clare began.

'Matteo will see to that.' Paola tugged her into the house.

'Matteo?'

'Guido's *maggiordomo*. And his wife, Benedetta, is the housekeeper.'

Clare found herself in a big, shadowy entrance hall with a flagged floor. At the far end, a wide stone staircase led the way to the upper floor, its harsh lines softened by a central strip of thick crimson carpet.

High, narrow windows admitted slanting pools of sunlight, and as she was whisked towards the stairs Clare noticed a number of double doors spaced at intervals around the hall. But before she could speculate where they might lead, she was halfway to the first floor.

'Are they the only staff?' she queried with slight breathlessness.

'*Dio*, no.' Paola gave a little laugh. 'There is a cook, and two maids, as well as Guido's driver—and his secretary. Then there is Alberto, the gardener, and the men who work for him. And Franco, who looks after the horses...'

'A cast of thousands,' Clare commented drily. 'I didn't realise there'd be horses here.'

'Guido likes them.' Paola's tone was offhand. 'When he was younger, of course, he played polo.'

'You don't ride?'

Paola shuddered dramatically. 'No—nor play tennis, although Guido wishes me to learn.'

Clare smiled. 'It's a terrific game. You might enjoy it.'

Paola tossed her head. 'Oh it is far too hot, and, besides, I do not like to run about. Although sometimes I swim in the pool,' she added on a note of self-congratulation.

The Marchese might have been right about Paola's lack of stamina after all, Clare thought wryly, following the younger girl along a broad gallery.

'Do you play tennis—and ride—and go for long walks?'

'Why—yes.'

'And you truly like these things?' Paola sighed gustily at Clare's affirmative nod. 'I shall never understand—never. But it's good, because you can be a companion for Guido, and I shall have some peace.'

But that's not the plan at all, Clare thought, appalled, and was about to say so when Paola announced, 'You are here,' and threw open a door with a flourish, allow-

ing Clare to walk past her into the biggest bedroom she'd
ever seen.

She had always considered that Violetta lived in a fair
amount of luxury, but now her eyes widened as she took
in the huge bed which dominated the room, its canopy
and curtains in ivory silk, and the matching coverlet ornamented with medallions exquisitely embroidered in
gold thread.

The rest of the furniture was correspondingly large,
and made from some dark, heavily carved wood, and the
far wall was occupied by tall shuttered windows giving
access on to a wide balcony with a delicate wrought-
iron balustrade.

The chill of the marble-tiled floor was relieved by
beautiful tapestry rugs in blue, green and gold.

The adjoining bathroom was equally glamorous, tiled
in grey and silver, with a sunken bath deep and wide
enough for multiple occupation. There were stacks of
white linen towels emblazoned with the Bartaldi family
crest, and mirrored shelves of toiletries.

'My room is further down the gallery, and Signora
Andreati will be placed next door to you,' Paola continued, as they returned to the bedroom. 'Do you think you
will be comfortable here?'

Clare drew a deep breath. 'More than just comfortable,' she said. 'It's all—quite amazing. I can hardly
believe it.'

Paola shrugged. 'It's old-fashioned. *Antiquato*,' she
said dismissively. 'And Guido refuses to change anything.' Her eyes brightened. 'You should see my stepmother's apartment in Rome. Now that is truly *elegante*—and so modern.'

She sighed, then pointed to a silken rope hanging beside the bed. 'If you need anything, ring the bell and

Filumena, one of the maids, will come. She will also unpack for you if you wish.'

Clare shook her head. 'I can manage my own unpacking. And I can't think of a thing that hasn't been provided already.

'Well, Guido will wish you to be contented.' Paola pulled a face. 'Whatever I may think about him, I cannot deny he is a good host. And I am pleased that he brought you so early—so that we can have breakfast together. Come down when you are ready, and we will eat.'

She walked to the door, then looked back, lowering her voice mysteriously. 'And later we will talk. Make plans. *Ciao.*' And she vanished, leaving Clare feeling winded, and slightly apprehensive.

To try and ensure that Paola had a say in her own future was one thing, but plotting with her, especially if Fabio was involved, was something else.

She thought, I'm going to have to be very careful.

But, in the meantime, she could enjoy herself a little. She took another long, pleasurable look round the room, her gaze coming speculatively to rest on the big bed, wondering if it was really as soft and luxurious as it appeared.

Well, there was only one way to find out, she decided gleefully.

She took a flying leap and landed in the middle of it, bouncing up and down to test the springs, which met the challenge nobly.

She turned over and lay voluptuously, lazily supine, her arms tossed wide, one leg slightly drawn up, staring at the silken canopy above her.

This, she thought dreamily, must be what it's like to float on a cloud. I shall sleep well in this bed. In fact, I could sleep right now. Just—drift away...

The tap on the door signalled the end of that particular dream, and the arrival of her luggage. What was the maid's name? Had Paola said Filumena? Yes, she was sure of it.

She called, 'Come in.' And, as the door opened, 'Please leave my bag by the *cassetone*, Filumena. I'll see to it later.'

'As you wish, *signorina*.' The amused drawl which responded had no feminine tone whatsoever.

Clare jack-knifed into an upright position, tugging down her rumpled skirt, shocked colour flooding her face as Guido walked across the room and deposited her bag by the chest of drawers.

'I am sorry to have startled you,' he went on. 'I brought your things myself so that I could make sure you had everything you needed.'

Clare swallowed. 'Yes—I—everything…' she managed.

She couldn't imagine what he must be thinking, finding her sprawled across a probably priceless bedspread like this.

He walked slowly across the room and stood at the foot of the bed, looking down at her, smiling faintly. 'You like the bed.'

It was a statement rather than a question, and Clare nodded mutely.

'This was the room my mother used when she came to stay here before her marriage, while my father was paying court to her.' His voice was almost meditative. 'It was considered to be a safe distance from his room, on the other side of the gallery, and besides, her mother was next door.

'But I have often wondered if, during the long, hot Umbrian afternoons, love did not sometimes find a way.

'It is, after all, a serious temptation to find yourself under the same roof as the one you desire—don't you think, Chiara?'

'I—I don't know.' Her mouth was dry, but her body was suddenly melting, stirred into arousal by the images he had created.

She could feel a trickle of sweat running down the valley between her breasts, as her nipples swelled uncontrollably into hard peaks against the clinging fabric of her top. The damp, potent heat between her thighs seemed to be spreading through her entire being, engulfing her. Prompting her to madness. To ruin.

Because some secret, atavistic wisdom was telling her that all she had to do was reach out a hand to him—draw him down beside her—and her body would be his.

She knew it as surely as she knew she must draw air into her lungs to breathe.

And, for a few, brief honeyed moments, he would belong to her, too. But only in the most basic, physical sense. There could never be any more to it than that.

Whereas she was offering him her heart and soul. The year's most unwanted gift, she realised with sudden, savage anguish.

And only she would ever know how close she had come to betraying her own pride and self-respect.

From somewhere, she found a voice. Cool, calm and almost collected. A stranger's. 'Those were other times, *signore*. And other people. Now if you'll excuse me, I'd like to unpack. Would you tell Paola that I'll join her in a minute?'

There was a silence, then he said quietly, 'It will be my pleasure.'

She did not watch him walk away. And she sensed rather than heard the door close behind him.

And even when she knew she was alone she did not move, but stayed where she was, crouched tensely on the bed, her arms wrapped round her body. As if remaining quiet and still would somehow shield her from disaster. From the danger she'd sensed in the first moment she saw him. The danger of total self-betrayal.

She said with a new and passionate intensity, 'I shall indeed have to be careful. Very careful.'

And shivered.

CHAPTER SEVEN

SHE could not, of course, stay where she was, hiding in her room, however much she might want to.

Out of the confusion of her thoughts, that much at least was plain.

Because to skulk ignominiously upstairs would be a complete give-away. An acknowledgement that he had got to her. Penetrated the guard she had thought virtually indestructible. Set her emotions in turmoil. And she could not allow him such a victory.

He had chosen Paola and he intended to marry her, and that was it. That was everything. Anything else was game-playing, probably because he was bored with his tepid courtship.

So, she had to fight him—but not by meeting fire with fire. She could see what a perilous course that might be. No, her best—her safest bet was a war of attrition. Following her own rules of play instead of being beguiled by his. Demonstrating politely, even smilingly, that she was totally indifferent to his lethal charm. That he couldn't reach her any more.

It might take time, but he would eventually get the message. He was an experienced, sophisticated man. A one-sided contest would soon hold little interest for him.

And for her, the real struggle would be with herself, she acknowledged painfully. Forcing herself to control her vulnerable senses—to subdue every female instinct she possessed.

And somehow she had to begin now. She had to walk

down that imposing staircase and join Guido Bartaldi and his family in the dining room for breakfast, and it would require every shred of composure in her being.

She dived into her travel bag and extracted a dress, straight-cut and businesslike in navy, with short sleeves and a discreetly rounded neck, adding low-heeled navy sandals. She brushed her hair back severely from her face, and confined it at the nape of her neck with a tortoiseshell barrette.

That was better, she thought, viewing herself critically in one of the full-length mirrors. She looked quiet and professional, and that was the image she needed to put over. It was an armour that had served her well in the past.

She drew a deep, steadying breath, then started downstairs. Matteo was waiting in the hall to conduct her to the dining room.

'*Grazie.*' She returned his smile. 'So many doors.'

'You will soon become accustomed, *signorina.*' He nodded. '*Si*, very soon you will be quite at home.'

Which was the last thing she wanted to hear.

But it helped that the dining room seemed full of people as he showed her in. She was able to smile round and return the polite chorus of '*Buongiornos*' which greeted her, and pretend to be unconscious of the tall figure standing by the window at the end of the room.

'So there you are. What an age you have been.' Paola came over to her, slipping an arm through hers. 'Everyone is waiting to meet you.' She led Clare over to the handsome older man she'd glimpsed outside the Villa Rosa. 'This is Guido's uncle, the Conte di Mantelli. May I present Chiara Marriot, who is to be my companion?'

'It is a pleasure, *signorina*. And one too long delayed.'

The Count's handshake was firm, and his face kind. 'But I have heard a great deal about you, of course.'

'I can't think that the Marchese can have found to say. After all, we hardly know each other.' Clare's tone was repressive, and he looked surprised.

'Guido? But I was referring to your godmother, the Signora Andreati. She has been my informant.'

'Oh,' Clare said in a hollow voice. 'I see.'

Well done, she berated herself silently. An own goal in the first minute.

She was horribly aware that Guido had heard every word of the little exchange, and was looking frankly amused.

She turned with something like relief to meet Tonio Lerucci, introduced by Paola with a casualness that bordered on rudeness.

He was younger than she'd imagined, and of medium height, with a charming smile that lit his dark monkey face.

'It is good to meet you, *signorina*. Let me get you some coffee.'

She thanked him, chatting lightly while she filled a plate from the display of cold meat, sausage and cheese on the massive sideboard, and took a hot roll from a covered basket proffered by a maid.

Guido had taken his seat at the head of the table, so she contrived to manouevre herself into a chair at the other end, finding herself next to the Count.

'So, *signorina*, what do you think of the Villa Minerva? Or is it too early to make a judgement?'

'By no means. I think it's—beautiful.' She glanced up at the exquisitely painted ceiling. 'That must be very old.'

'Nearly four hundred years,' he agreed. 'As you see,

it is a representation of Leda and the god Zeus who came to her in the guise of a swan.' He pointed. 'And there is the goddess Hera, watching jealously.'

'As she had to do so often,' Clare said drily. 'The painting's in wonderful condition.'

'It has undergone certain restoration work, as most of the house's treasures have done.' He turned his head towards the Marchese. 'I am telling Signorina Marriot, Guido, that you are an excellent guardian of your heritage.' He nodded. 'Your son will be a fortunate man.'

Clare, wincing inwardly, saw Paola look up with a mutinous scowl, and hastily intervened with a question about the date of the present house, which the Count was happy to answer.

He was clearly an enthusiast, and very knowledgeable, and after a while Clare forgot her self-consciousness in the sheer pleasure of listening to him.

During their conversation, she learned that he had been married to Guido's aunt, but had been a widower for nearly five years.

'To our sorrow, we had no children,' he said. 'So Guido was always more than a nephew to us, and, since I have been alone, he has made sure I continue to be part of his family.' He smiled faintly. 'He has a keen sense of his obligations, although, admittedly, he has waited longer to marry than his father would have wished.'

Clare bit her lip. 'Perhaps he's been waiting for his bride to grow up,' she suggested awkwardly.

'Or maybe he wished to be sure that she was the one woman to fill his life,' the Count said gently. 'He has made no secret of desiring a marriage as happy as that of his parents.'

Then why is he marrying Paola? Clare bit back the

question. It was not her place to ask, she told herself raggedly. And, if he was determined enough, he could probably salvage something from such an ill-matched relationship, anyway.

Breakfast over, Clare found herself commandeered by Paola, on the pretext that she wished to show her the gardens.

'Fine,' she said. 'But then we must do some work. After all, I'm here primarily to give you language lessons.'

Paola pulled a face. 'School. Always it is more school with Guido.'

'Well, it's important that you should be able to talk to foreign clients with him,' Clare said reasonably.

Paola giggled. 'But that is not going to happen, silly one. And Fabio speaks only Italian, so you can just pretend to give me lessons.'

I think, Clare mused wearily, as she followed the younger girl into the sunlit grounds, that I already have as much pretence in my life as I can handle.

In spite of her misgivings, Clare found her first day at the Villa Minerva passing more tranquilly than she could have hoped.

She toured the gardens with Paola, turning a partially deaf ear to the torrent of half-formed and generally unworkable plans for her future that the younger girl assailed her with.

The villa's grounds were extensive and immaculately kept, and Clare, who loved plants, and had always worked alongside her father in their own garden, would have liked to have absorbed it all in peace.

But, as this was clearly impossible, every so often she tried to introduce a note of sceptical and practical reality by asking what Fabio did for a living, where they would live after they were married, and how their bills would be paid. But Paola was inclined to dismiss all that as irrelevant.

'All that matters,' she declared passionately, 'is our love for each other. And, besides, I shall have money when I'm older. I shall just have to make Guido give some of it to me now.'

Clare raised her brows. 'After you've made a fool of him by running off with Fabio?' She shook her head. 'I wouldn't count on it.'

'Ah,' Paola said triumphantly. 'But he will not wish it to be known that I have fooled him. Therefore, for the sake of his pride, he will do what I want, so that people will think he does not care.'

In which there was a certain twisted logic, Clare was forced to admit.

She said, 'Well, I hope everything works out for the best. Now, can you tell me the names of these flowers in English?'

But this Paola could not do, cheerfully admitting she didn't know what they were called in Italian either.

'Instead, we will go down to the pool and swim a little,' she announced.

'Paola, I'm here to work, not vacation.'

Paola pouted. 'But this is only the first day. And Guido will not know. He and Tonio will be shut up in his study all morning, talking about farms and vineyards and the olive crop. All we need to do is avoid Zio Cesare, who is boring.'

'He's nothing of the sort,' Clare said roundly. 'I was fascinated by what he was telling me about the villa.'

Paola gave her a stare of sheer incredulity. 'Chiara—you like to hear about Etruscans—and architecture—and the school of Raphael?' She flung her hands in the air. 'Then there is no hope for you.'

'No,' Clare agreed quietly. 'I don't suppose there is.'

In the event, they had the pool entirely to themselves. Clare was about to go back to the house to get her swimsuit, but Paola directed her to the stone-built cabins, on a cypress-sheltered terrace overlooking the water, which served as showers and changing rooms, and told her that there was always a supply of spare swimsuits and towels for guests.

Most of those on offer seemed to be bikinis considerably briefer than her own, so Clare opted for a one-piece in a deep bronze colour.

It wasn't really suitable either, she thought grimly, being cut far too high in the leg and low in the neck, and fitting her like a second skin to boot.

Paola, she discovered, had simply discarded the cotton shift she'd been wearing to reveal a costume that consisted of a black thong and two minute circles of material that barely covered her nipples.

Really, Clare thought wearily, it hardly seemed worth the effort.

But the pool itself was wonderful, a great oval of gleaming turquoise water surrounded by tiled sunbathing terraces.

She walked to the edge and submerged a foot gingerly. The water felt terrific—cool, but refreshing. She poised herself, then dived in, swiftly and cleanly, completing three lengths without pausing.

'You are crazy,' Paola told her severely, as Clare hauled herself out on to the side and wrung the water from her hair. 'Such exercise cannot be good. You will develop big muscles—like a man.'

Clare grinned. 'I'll take that chance.' She towelled

herself down, then stretched out on an adjacent lounger to Paola's.

The morning was still, and would soon be very hot. After a few desultory remarks about her longing to hear from Fabio again, Paola drifted into silence, and then into a light doze.

But Clare had her thoughts to keep her awake. She was beginning to think she had bitten off more than she could chew where Paola was concerned. Perhaps it would have been wiser simply to tell Guido Bartaldi that, in spite of everything, his future wife was still planning to elope with her fortune-hunter, and let him deal with the situation in his own way.

If he fully appreciated Paola's determination to be rid of him, he might even abandon the whole idea of marrying her. Or it might make him equally determined to win her over.

He wasn't a man to easily surrender his own will, and his mind was set on Paola.

She sighed, and sat up restlessly, swinging her legs off the lounger. She was in no mood to lie around brooding.

She said softly, 'Paola? I'm going up to the house to unpack, and make some notes about the lessons. I'll see you at lunch.'

The only reply was a sleepy murmur which might have meant anything.

Draping her towel round her shoulders, Clare walked up the stone steps between the banks of shrubs towards the changing cabin.

The air was full of scent, and busy with the hum of insects. She drew a deep breath, and became suddenly aware of another less agreeable aroma.

Somewhere in the vicinity someone was smoking a cigarette.

Frowning, she glanced along the row of cypresses, and saw a young man standing between them, leaning on a hoe, the offending cigarette between faintly smiling lips as he stared down at the pool area. Wearing earth-stained jeans, and bare-chested, he was good-looking in an obvious way, and, if Clare was any judge, perfectly aware of his own attractions.

One of the gardeners, she thought, biting her lip, taking a sly look at Paola sunbathing, and so engrossed he hadn't heard her approach.

She said in icy Italian, 'Have you no work to do?'

He started, and turned to look at her. 'I'm sorry, *signorina*.' His tone was polite, even ingratiating, but his eyes were insolent, sliding swiftly and appraisingly over her body, making her regret even more the revealing nature of her swimsuit. 'I am having my break. I did not realise there was anyone at the pool.'

Clare lifted her chin, giving him a sceptical look. 'Well, now that you know, go and have your break somewhere else,' she said crisply.

'*Si, signorina.* At once. Naturally. Forgive me. I have not worked here very long, and I did not understand... I—I need this job, *signorina*. I am Marco's cousin. He spoke for me to Signor Lerucci.'

Clare didn't want to hear any more. Pulling the towel more tightly round her shoulders, she started up the steps again. Then paused, as she was struck by the sudden conviction that, despite his grovelling protestations, he was still standing there, laughing at her behind her back. She swung round to challenge him, but apart from the discarded cigarette, burning on the ground, there was no sign of him.

She thought, good riddance, and went on up to the cabin.

At some point, she thought, stepping under the shower, she would have a word with Tonio Lerucci about this Marco's precious cousin.

She peeled off the borrowed swimsuit, and wrapped another towel around her, sarong-style, as she went to her cubicle to dress.

Only to realise when she got in there that she'd made a mistake somehow. Because the dress hanging from the peg bore no resemblance to her navy linen camouflage.

Except that it was also blue, a vibrant shade, like lapis lazuli, with the added sheen of silk.

She was about to go and search the other cubicles when she realised that the pile of neatly folded underwear on the stool in the corner was certainly hers. And at the same moment she saw that the strange dress had a piece of paper pinned to its filmy drift of skirt.

She detached it, and, lips compressed, read the message.

'Forgive me,' it ran, 'but it is clearly time the navy dress was consigned to a well-deserved oblivion. I hope its replacement will give you pleasure.' No signature, but the initials 'G.B.'—just in case she was in the slightest doubt over who was responsible for this—this outrage.

She said aloud, her voice shaking, 'How dare he? How dare he do this—presume to criticise me?'

She dismissed from her mind the fact that the navy dress had been the one she liked least in her entire wardrobe, and that she'd chosen to wear it solely as a gesture.

And she ignored the sly voice in her head reminding her that all the Marchese had done was recognise what she was up to and respond with his own telling form of provocation.

'He has no right,' she stormed on. 'I'm damned if I'll wear his bloody dress. I'll see him in hell before...'

And stopped right there, as she realised the other options open to her. She could either climb back into that damp and clammy swimsuit, or walk around in her undies. And neither alternative held any appeal for her.

On the other hand, Guido Bartaldi could not be allowed to get away with this high-handed behaviour.

Reluctantly, Clare donned her underwear, and slid the new dress over her head. She was half hoping it wouldn't fit, although that would mean having to wear her towel back to the house.

But of course it moulded itself to her slender curves perfectly, the low, rounded neckline giving just a hint of the swell of her breasts and the folds of the skirt whispering silkily around her slim legs. The colour looked good on her too, she admitted grudgingly.

But somehow that made everything worse—implying that he had some in-built intimate knowledge of her—her size, her shape, even her skin tones.

She found she was shivering, and shook herself impatiently. She needed to march into this confrontation, not hang back, trembling.

But when she got back to the villa, she was halted in her tracks by the realisation that she had no idea where Guido was. And there was no kindly major-domo waiting to point the way, either.

As she stood, debating her next move, a door to the rear of the massive hallway opened and Tonio Lerucci appeared. He did not see Clare at once, because he was still looking back over his shoulder into the room he'd just vacated, and apparently finishing a conversation with its occupant.

When he turned, his brows lifted in an open surprise. 'Signorina Marriot?' He laughed. 'Forgive me. Almost I did not recognise you.'

Clare smiled sweetly back. 'Don't worry about it, *signore*. Sometimes I hardly know myself.' She paused. 'Is our lord and master alone? I'd like to speak to him.'

'It will be his pleasure, *signorina*,' Tonio returned gallantly.

Don't count on it, thought Clare, briskly obeying his polite indication that she should walk past him into the study.

It was a large book-lined room, and rather dark, the low ornamental ceiling of moulded plaster supported on stone pillars. But its traditional formality was offset by the French doors standing open to the sunlit garden beyond, and the very modern desk with its bank of computer equipment. And, not least, by Guido Bartaldi, totally casual in shorts and an unbuttoned shirt in thin cotton, who was perched on the edge of the desk, long legs much in evidence, as he studied the information on the screen in front of him.

As she closed the door behind her, Clare said clearly and coldly, 'I'd like a word with you, *signore*.'

'But not a pleasant one, it seems.' He lifted his head and subjected her to a long stare which held a measure of frank appreciation. 'I thought perhaps you had come to thank me.'

'To thank you?' Her voice rose sightly. 'For what? For insulting me?'

'In what way?'

'You know perfectly well.' She took a fold of the

dress between thumb and forefinger and held it out with distaste. 'With—this.'

'I am sorry you don't like it,' he said, after a pause. 'But we can always find something else. Is it the colour which offends you, or the fabric?'

'Neither.' Clare bit down hard on her lip. 'It's—the concept that you should buy me clothes.'

He looked surprised. 'I supply uniforms for all the staff in this house. None of them complain.'

She gasped. 'You call—this a uniform? You must be joking.'

'Well, let us compromise and call it work clothing,' he said smoothly.

Clare drew a deep breath. 'Let us do nothing of the kind,' she said stonily. 'In my previous employment I've always worn my own clothes.'

'And did they all resemble the garment you wore to breakfast—or was that a special choice?'

The note of amusement in his voice did nothing to improve Clare's temper. Nor the fact that he'd seen so effortlessly through her little ploy.

She said tautly, 'I'm sorry, naturally, if my fashion sense doesn't meet your exacting standards, but I still prefer to wear my own things. And I'd like my navy dress back, please.'

'Ah,' he said, after a pause. 'That could be a problem.'

'I fail to see why.'

'There are several reasons,' Guido said calmly. 'Firstly my uncle, who is, you understand, an art historian, and whose sense of the aesthetic was crucified this morning by your decision to shroud yourself in an ill-fitting sack. He's no longer so young, and I must consider his feelings. You see how it is?'

'No,' Clare said roundly. 'I don't.'

'Then there is the actual fate of the dress itself,' he went on musingly. 'I told Filumena, who made the substitution, to burn it. I am sure she has obeyed me by now.'

Clare stared at him. 'You—burned my dress?' she asked with ominous calm.

'It seemed the easiest solution.' He nodded. 'Otherwise I could foresee it would continue to haunt us all during your time here.'

'But this is an outrage.' Her voice shook. 'You can't do this.'

'Unfortunately, it is already done.' He paused. 'Although I cannot pretend my regrets are sincere. Not when you are standing here in front of me, wearing the replacement.'

He swung himself down from the desk. '*Dio*, Chiara.' There was a sudden fierce, uneven note in his voice. 'Don't you know how beautiful you are?'

Clare looked down at the floor, detaching herself from the dark gaze consuming her, feeling her throat close.

'You have no right to speak to me like that,' she said quietly. 'No right to say those things to any woman except Paola.'

'There is no need to say it to Paola,' he retorted harshly. 'She is already secure in the power of her own attraction. But you, *mia bella*, are a different matter. And I am not blind.'

'You promised you wouldn't talk like this,' she said shakily. 'You said if I came here, I'd be safe.'

'And so you are, Chiara.' His voice was husky—strained. 'Safer than you will ever know. But I never pretended it would be easy. Or that I would not be tempted.'

'I'd better go.' She still did not dare to look at him.

'If I must keep this dress, *signore*, then I insist that you deduct its cost from my salary. No one pays for my clothes except myself.'

'As you wish.' The words were clipped.

'As for Paola,' she continued, with a kind of desperation to have the last word, and leave the confrontation on a winning note, 'she may not be as secure as you think. You see—she knows about your lady in Siena.'

As she turned to the door, she was aware of movement behind her, then her arm was grasped and she was whirled round to face him.

'What are you talking about?' he demanded harshly. 'What has she told you?'

'Not the details.' Clare tried unsuccessfully to free herself. 'Just that you had another interest.'

'And you believed her?'

'Why not?' she countered recklessly. 'After all, Marchese, there hasn't been much in your conduct so far to convince me that fidelity would ever be high on your list of priorities.'

The moment she'd said it, she was sorry. But it was too late. She saw his face darkening, the skin tautening over the elegant bone structure. Saw the cold, angry glitter in his eyes.

There was ice in his voice. 'If that is what you think, Chiara, then why should I hesitate any longer?'

With one swift, compelling gesture, he pulled Clare into his arms, grinding her body against his. Forcing her into sudden awareness that he was not merely angry, but strongly aroused too. The stinging heat of his need penetrated the thin layers of clothing that separated them as if they no longer existed, and Clare's breath caught in her throat as the roughness of his chest hair grazed her breasts.

For a long moment he stared down at her, scanning her dilated eyes and vulnerable mouth, the anger and coldness fading from his face to be replaced by a gentler, almost diffident expression, while his hand slowly lifted to tangle in her still-damp blonde hair, forbidding movement, holding her captive for his kiss.

She knew that she should make some protest—some attempt, at least, to push him away—but she couldn't do it. She was too excited by his nearness, every nerve-ending in her skin tingling in anticipation of the touch of his hands, uncovering her. Discovering her.

The whimper slowly uncoiling in her throat was one of longing, not outrage.

He bent his head, and his mouth began to touch hers, lightly, almost feverishly, his tongue flickering like flame between her parted lips.

For a brief moment Clare was passive in his arms, letting the first sharp stirrings of pleasure begin to build deep within her being.

Then, as his kiss deepened, she responded, her mouth moving on his with shy ardour, and heard him murmur quietly in satisfaction.

His fingertips were stroking the nape of her neck, under the fall of her hair, then sliding down to caress the line of her throat, the curve of her shoulder.

Her nipples ached as they pressed against the confines of her dress. Her legs felt too weak to support her, and she was trembling, melting inside, her body electric with the shock of desire.

Her hands slid inside the open edges of his shirt to find his shoulders, and cling to them as if she was drowning.

Guido tipped her back over his arm, laying a trail of kisses down her throat, then slowly brushing his lips across the first soft swell of her breasts, and a tiny sob of need rose in her throat. The beating of her heart sounded like distant thunder.

Only it had been joined, with brutal suddenness, by a very different pounding.

The sound, Clare realised, of someone knocking at the study door. As Guido straightened, frowning, she freed herself from his slackened grasp and stepped backwards, pressing the palms of her hands to her burning face, and trying to control her flurried breathing.

Guido called, 'Who is there?'

'Matteo, *signore*, to tell you that Signora Andreati has arrived. Her car is outside at this moment.'

'*Grazie*, Matteo. I will be with you immediately. And inform my uncle, please.'

He looked at Clare, his expression cool—even remote. 'Your godmother's timing is impeccable, *mia bella*. She has saved both of us from a terrible mistake.' He paused. 'I am going to greet her now, but you may prefer to go into the garden. I will send one of the maids to find you in a little while.'

'Yes.' Her voice was barely audible. 'That might be—best.'

She went across to the French windows, almost running. Stumbling a little.

She thought she heard him say, 'Chiara,' but she didn't stop or turn. Just kept going, out into the dazzle of the sunlight, her bottom lip caught painfully in her teeth and the phrase 'a terrible mistake' reverberating over and over again in her head.

CHAPTER EIGHT

PART of her wanted to die of shame. But another, and more realistic part of her knew that a life in which she'd never again feel his arms round her or taste his kisses would be total desolation anyway.

I could survive that—just, she thought. What I can't bear is that very soon I'll be leaving here—and I'll never see him again. Never hear his voice, or see his mouth curve into that slow, amused smile.

It was as if she'd been afforded a glimpse of Paradise, then had it taken away for ever. And that was the most devastating realisation of her entire life.

It was useless to argue that she and Guido Bartaldi had known each other only a matter of days, and that all she was suffering from was a severe case of physical attraction, which could soon be cured.

Her heart told her unequivocally that for her it went much deeper than that. That she wanted to spend the rest of her life with him—laughing with him, fighting the occasional battle with him, making him happy as she knew only she could.

Except that wasn't the way life worked out. Because Guido had his own plans, and they did not include herself. Unless she was content to exist on the margin of his life, like the woman in Siena.

Clearly he saw no reason why his private life could not be conducted on two levels. Which was why he planned to marry a pretty girl with whom he hardly shared a thought, while conducting other more fulfilling

liaisons at a safe distance. The cynicism of it—and the
sadness—made her want to weep, even though she knew
she should really despise him.

But she couldn't.

'Fool,' she lambasted herself. 'Sad, pathetic idiot.'

She'd found a secluded bench under a flowering
hedge a long way from the house, and she crouched
there, her arms hugged protectively round her body,
deathly cold in spite of the sun's heat.

Telling herself that Guido would not repeat his 'terrible mistake' and that she'd be safe from any further
advances from him was poor comfort. It would not save
her from hungering for him, she thought drearily. But at
least it might leave her with the tatters of her self-
respect.

She glanced at her watch and got reluctantly to her
feet. She'd been missing for nearly two hours, and
lunchtime was approaching. She didn't want search par-
ties being dispatched for her.

She'd been in too much emotional turmoil to take note
of the exact route to her refuge, but it hardly mattered
as all the paths in the grounds would lead back to the
villa.

But not necessarily to the part she knew, she discovered, as she emerged into a narrow cedar-lined avenue
which took her only to a small Romanesque building
with a *campanile* beside it, which she supposed must be
the Bartaldi family chapel.

The house, she saw, was some distance away to her
right, and she'd come out at the rear of it.

She checked, shading her eyes as she looked up at the
elaborate stone frontage of the chapel. Some of the fig-
ures of saints that ornamented it looked as if they had
seen better days, and some guttering was hanging loose.

Wondering what it was like inside, she tried the handle of the heavy wooden door, half expecting it to be locked, but it opened easily and she went in.

The interior was dark, most of the light coming from a round stained glass window above the altar which had been partly boarded up. The smell of incense lingered in the air, along with the more pungent odour of dust, but none of the candles were lit, and there was a downbeat air of disuse about the place which disappointed her.

She was turning to go when a door at the side of the sanctuary opened and Tonio Lerucci came into view, carrying a sheaf of papers.

He paused in obvious astonishment when he saw Clare. 'Signorina Marriot—what are you doing here?'

Clare shrugged. 'I like old churches. Am I trespassing?'

'No, no,' he said hastily. 'At least not if circumstances were normal. But you see the chapel and, even more, the *campanile* were damaged during the last earthquake, and we cannot be certain how safe they are.'

'But you're here,' Clare pointed out.

He laughed. 'Yes, but I am not an honoured guest of the Bartaldi. I'm here to make a preliminary inspection before the architect comes next week to assess what will need to be done to restore the chapel again.'

'So it's going to be repaired.' Clare looked round again. 'I'm glad. It doesn't look too bad. Just neglected.'

'I hope not, but we cannot tell until the actual structure is examined. The *campanile*, I think, will have to be demolished, but perhaps the repairs here will not be too extensive.' He grinned. 'If they are, I can see Guido becoming very impatient.'

Clare followed him out, and waited while he locked

the door. 'I didn't realise he was so religious.' She tried to keep her tone light.

'As to that, like most of us, he does his best,' Tonio said, shrugging. 'But the restoration of the chapel is close to his heart as he intends to be married there, and soon.'

'Oh,' Clare said in a hollow voice, as sudden pain transfixed her. 'I—didn't know.'

'Not many people do. It is quite a recent decision.'

'Does Paola know?' Clare strove to keep her voice calm. 'Because I'd have thought his bride should have some say in the matter.'

A couple of Tonio's papers fluttered to the ground, and he bent to retrieve them. 'No doubt he will choose his own moment for that,' he said vaguely. 'Maybe it would be best to mention nothing.'

'Of course.' Clare smiled tautly. 'I hope she'll find it a pleasant surprise.'

'The Marchese Bartaldi's wife will always have every reason for happiness,' was the formal reply.

Oops, thought Clare. Avoid any hint of criticism when speaking of revered employer. I expect I already have a black mark for steaming in there this morning. It must have been obvious I was spoiling for a fight.

In a hurried change of subject, she asked how many people worked on the Bartaldi estates, and was shocked by his answer.

'That many?' She swallowed. 'And do you know them all?'

'I hope so. You must understand, *signorina*, that many generations of the same families have worked here.'

'I see.' Her tone was thoughtful. 'So, if I said Marco's cousin, you'd know who I meant?'

He frowned slightly. 'I might not be able to put a face to him at once. Why do you ask?'

'Oh, I came across him earlier today, working in the garden.' She paused. 'He's quite—spectacular. You wouldn't overlook him very easily.'

'Then he does not resemble Marco, who is like a mouse,' he said drily. 'You disapprove of him, *signorina*?'

'Oh, please, won't you call me Clare?' She smiled at him. 'After all, we both work for the Marchese,' she added with a touch of constraint.

He hesitated oddly, then made her a slight bow. 'As you wish—Clare. But we were speaking of Marco's cousin.'

'Yes.' She bit her lip. 'He was hanging round the pool area, and there was just something—although I expect I'm being unfair, and he's a very good gardener.'

'Yet he does not feature on the estate roll,' Tonio said musingly. 'Perhaps the head gardener hired him as casual labour. I shall enquire.'

'Oh, dear,' she sighed. 'I hope I haven't got him into trouble.'

'No, no,' he soothed. 'At busy times there are always extra people working for the estate. It is nothing.'

I hope so, Clare thought, as he stood back politely to let her precede him into the house. And now for the next ordeal...

'Carissima,' Violetta exclaimed reproachfully as Clare entered the dining room. 'Where have you been? We were beginning to think you were lost.'

Clare coloured faintly, sharply aware of Guido's unsmiling scrutiny fixed on her from the other side of the room.

'I was—enjoying the garden, and lost track of time,' she returned, bending to kiss her godmother's scented cheek before sliding into the chair next to her.

'And not alone, I see,' Violetta whispered, giving her an arch look as Tonio took his place further down the table with a quiet apology. She looked Clare over approvingly. 'What a beautiful dress, my dear. I don't think I've seen it before.'

'It—it's the first time I've worn it,' Clare returned, helping herself from the tureen of vegetable soup.

'So, *cara*, how goes it with the little Paola?' Violetta was eating her own soup with evident enjoyment. 'Well, it seems. She looks—radiant.'

Surprised, Clare saw that the younger girl was laughing and talking vivaciously to Cesare di Mantelli.

'She's not going to be my easiest assignment,' she returned quietly. 'She simply hasn't any wish to learn any of the things I can teach her. I think she plans to rely on charm to see her through.' She paused. 'If I can't persuade her to buckle down soon, I'll give up the job. Otherwise I'll be taking the Marchese's money under false pretences.'

'I think he has plenty to spare,' Violetta said calmly. 'So I would not worry too much.' She gave Clare a measuring look. 'How do you like working for him, *mia cara*?'

'Not very much.' Clare put down her soup spoon. 'In fact I mean to keep out of his way from now on.'

'I imagine he can be demanding,' Violetta conceded. 'But such charm.' She cast her eyes to heaven. 'And you have the future to think of, dear one. Any association with the Bartaldi would be bound to bring its own rewards.'

A lifetime of heartache was hardly a reward, Clare

thought wretchedly, giving a constrained smile and murmuring something in reply.

When lunch was over, and Violetta was ensconced on the terrace with her coffee, and the Count di Mantelli for company, she sought out Paola.

'I thought we might walk to the village,' she suggested. 'It will give us the chance to practise some English conversation.'

'But there is nothing in the village,' Paola objected instantly. 'And it is too far to walk in the heat of the day. Besides, I am already getting a headache. I spent too much time in the sun this morning. I am going to take a siesta.'

'I see,' Clare said levelly. 'In that case I'd better talk to the Marchese and tell him there's no point in my remaining here.'

Paola's eyes widened. 'But you cannot do that,' she muttered. 'I need you. You know that.'

'But my salary is being paid by the Marchese,' Clare reminded her. 'And I have to start earning it. Which I can't do unless you co-operate.' She looked at her watch. 'Suppose we meet here on the terrace at four.' She gave the younger girl an encouraging smile. 'I'll try and make our lessons fun. Not like being in school at all.'

Paola's look said she was unconvinced, but she gave unwilling agreement to the plan.

'But it is such a waste of time,' she hissed as she departed. 'When we both know these lessons will not be needed.'

Clare sighed, and turned back to find her godmother and offer to stroll round the gardens with her, only to see her walking off with the Count down one of the paths.

'They make a handsome couple, don't you think?'

Tonio came to stand beside her.

She stared at him. 'You're not serious?'

'Why not?' He spread his hands. 'The Conte is an attractive, vigorous man—and a widower. The Signora is a beautiful, cultivated woman—and a widow.'

'Yes,' Clare said. 'And she values her independence—as I do.'

He laughed. 'Then you have come to the wrong place, Clare. For hundreds of years men and women have courted each other here at the Villa Minerva. It is a place for love—for happiness. For coming together. And there is soon to be a wedding here,' he added, smiling. 'Such an occasion puts ideas into other people's heads. Reminds them that it is not good to be alone.'

'I don't agree. Sometimes in your own company is the only safe place to be.' Out of the corner of her eye, Clare saw a tall figure approaching. 'Excuse me, please,' she added hastily. 'I have to go and make some notes about Paola's English lesson.'

'You really intend to teach her?' He sounded astonished.

'Of course,' she said. 'There's no other reason for me to be here.'

She turned away, intending to make for the house, only to be halted by Guido's, 'One moment Chiara. I wish to speak to you.'

Reluctantly, she turned and came back, noting that Tonio had already made a discreet exit.

'Is this strictly necessary?' She lifted her chin. 'I have—things to do.'

'Then they must wait.' His voice held a touch of grimness. 'We need to talk about this morning.'

'I'd rather not.' She stared down at the ancient flag-stones.

'There are still things that need to be said.' He paused. 'You must understand that I did not intend—that to happen.' His mouth tightened. 'I am not accustomed to having the conduct of my personal life challenged in that way. I—lost my temper.'

'Yes.' Her voice was barely audible.

'It was—an error of judgement on my part—which I deeply regret,' Guido went on, his voice low and intense. 'When you came here, I offered you certain safeguards. I have failed to keep my part of the bargain, and for that I ask your pardon.'

'You don't have to apologise.' She kept her voice steady. 'You already made your position—perfectly clear. And I was also to blame. I lost my temper too.' She even forced a small, bleak smile. 'As you said, it was a mistake. But not a fatal one. We can put it behind us. Pretend it never happened.'

He said quietly, 'Can you do that, Chiara? Can you deceive yourself—like that? Because I do not think it is possible. I do not believe my memory will allow itself to be cheated in that way.'

Her nails dug into the palms of her hands. 'Please, *signore*, don't take this so seriously. It's really not important. Men make advances to women who work for them every day.' She shrugged. 'It's an occupational hazard.'

'Not,' he said thinly, 'in my organisation.'

She swallowed. 'Then let's agree that we both got angry, and behaved out of character, and resolve to operate on a more businesslike footing in future.' She hesitated. 'Unless you'd prefer me to leave?'

'No,' he said. 'Not now. Not yet. Although I see it may become necessary sooner than I thought,' he added quietly.

He held out his hand. 'So—a new beginning, Chiara?'

After a momentary pause, she put her hand into his, and felt the swift, warm pressure of his fingers.

The kind of brief, impersonal contact which was all she could expect from now on, she acknowledged forlornly as he released her.

She said with forced brightness, 'If you'll excuse me now, Marchese.'

'Go in peace, *signorina*.' She could hear the undercurrent of amusement as he imitated her own formality.

As she turned away, his voice reached her softly, almost tauntingly. 'But I do not apologise for the dress, Chiara. How could I, when you look so beautiful? A dream of desire for any man's eyes.'

His words shivered through her being, tapping the turbulent well of emotion he had already created. Clare saw the sunlit day splinter into sparkling fragments as she fought back her tears. Battled with the yearning to go back to him, whatever the cost.

'You don't play fair, *signore*,' she threw back huskily, keeping her back resolutely turned to him. 'Has no one ever told you that?'

'Many people, *mia cara*.' There was a quietly implacable note now. 'And they will also tell you I always play to win.'

She said coolly and clearly, 'Then it's fortunate that your prize is Paola, and not myself, *signore*, or you'd lose. Good afternoon.'

And, forcing her shaking legs to obey her, she walked into the house, and up to the fragile security of her room.

She tried to rest, to sink down into the softness of the big bed and close out the world for a while, but she couldn't relax. Her mind and body were too much on edge. And even when she closed her eyes, Guido's image seemed to be stamped inside her eyelids, offering her no escape.

But this was the wrong room in which to evade thoughts of passion, she realised unhappily, recalling what he'd said about his own parents, and their long-ago clandestine lovemaking.

She'd hung the blue dress in a corner of the wardrobe. She wouldn't wear it again, but she couldn't bear to throw it away either. At least not yet. One day there would be a time when she would look back on this Umbrian summer with nothing more than a rueful smile, and then she could get rid of it as just another unwanted souvenir. At least, she prayed it would be so.

In the meantime, she had to deal with the sultry heat of the afternoon, the heavy quiet which had descended on the entire household, admixed with the scent of the flowers from the garden below and the drowsy hum of insects.

It was not, she thought grimly, the kind of atmosphere for solitude. It was all too evocative of whispered words, stifled laughter, and the slow, languorous movement of bodies reaching a familiar and precious attunement. A time when love was reaffirmed, and babies were made...

With a small, stifled sound, Clare swung herself off the bed and went into the bathroom, discarding her underwear on the way. She turned the temperature of the shower to cool, and let it rain down on her until she was half-blinded, half-deafened.

Seizing a handful of towels, she blotted the moisture from her body, then rubbed her hair so fiercely that her scalp tingled.

Wrapping a dry bath sheet around her, sarong-style, she wandered over to the window and looked out across the shimmering landscape to the dark green hills crowding behind.

There would be shade in those trees, she thought wistfully. And space where she could be alone without feeling suffocated. And a walk might clear her mind, as well as giving her something to do before she met up with Paola.

Quickly, she donned white broderie anglaise briefs, topping them with crisp turquoise cotton pants and a matching loose shirt, picked up the wide-brimmed straw hat she wore for sightseeing, and let herself quietly out of her room.

When she'd been looking at the chapel that morning, she'd noticed there was a gate in the wall at its rear which seemed to allow access straight on to the hills, and she made for that.

It opened with a squeal of protesting hinges that cut the somnolent afternoon like a knife. Wincing, she slipped through, and dragged it shut again behind her.

There were several paths to choose from, one of which actually skirted the hill, but Clare decided to head up a well-worn but steep track which zig-zagged its way up to the trees.

She was soon in their shadow, and glad of it as the gradient increased sharply. From this point, she saw, rough steps had been cut into the rocky ground and rope looped alongside, between the trees to assist in the climb.

She went up at a steady pace, only realising how high she had reached when she paused for a breather and saw the Villa Minerva and its gardens laid out beneath her like a child's dolls' house.

How lovely it looked, she thought, her throat tightening. And how hauntingly, achingly familiar it had become in such a brief time.

She resolved that before she left she would come up here with her camera, and get a more tangible picture than the one she would always carry in her heart.

In the meantime, she was curious to know where these endless steps were leading. They were obviously well used, demonstrating that visitors to the villa were hardy souls.

Maybe you go on climbing till you get altitude problems, then come down again, she thought, her mouth twisting.

But, after another five minutes' climbing, the ground levelled out suddenly, and the path divided.

'Decisions, decisions,' she muttered, hesitating. Then, invading the heavy stillness of the afternoon, she heard the distant sound of running water coming from the direction of the left-hand fork, and the choice was made for her.

Ahead of her, the trees were thinning out, and she glimpsed the solid grey of rock. She'd picked a cul-de-sac, it seemed, and for a moment she was tempted to turn back.

Moments later, she stepped out into what seemed to be a pool of sunlight. The narrow plateau she'd been traversing had opened out into a deep, grassy bowl, bounded by a wall of solid rock soaring high above her. She'd walked straight into a fold of the hills, she thought.

And there was the water she'd heard, a tiny, fierce stream bursting out of the wall of stone into a channel of its own making, until it was lost again in a deep fissure at the foot of the rock.

But she was wrong to think she'd have this isolated spot to herself. Someone was already there, waiting as she had been over all the centuries in a niche cut in the rock. A statue of a woman in a pleated robe, wearing a war-helmet, with a spear in her hand and a bird like an owl perched on her shoulder. Even the crudeness of the carving could not disguise the power of the figure, or the calm stone eyes looking down on the mortal girl who'd stumbled on her shrine.

'Minerva, the warrior-goddess of wisdom.'

Clare started violently at the quietly spoken words, as Guido walked out of the sheltering trees and came to her side.

'And my house's greatest treasure,' he added. 'No jewel, no piece of gold ever compared with this.' He smiled. 'I knew she would draw you here.'

Clare swallowed, conscious of the swift thunder of her pulses. 'Did you follow me?' she demanded, lifting her chin defiantly.

'No,' he said. 'I was here before you. But when I heard you coming, I went away, because I wanted you to discover her for yourself. And you did.'

'I just came out for a walk,' Clare said defensively. 'I didn't mean to intrude on your privacy. And I had no idea that this place or the statue existed. Your uncle never mentioned her when he was talking about the villa's history.'

'No,' he said. 'We rarely speak of her openly for security's sake. And very few who come to the house find their way this far.'

Clare looked back at the stone figure. 'How old is she?'

'Two thousand—three thousand years. No one is sure. But she was well hidden in her shrine. Rocks and stones had been piled up to hide her, probably when the barbarians invaded. Then, five hundred years ago, there was an earthquake, and she was found again. And there she has stood ever since.'

'Even through the last earthquake?' Clare shook her head. 'Wouldn't she be safer in a museum.'

'Perhaps, but my family have always fought to keep their Minerva here in her own sanctuary. The legend says the house of Bartaldi will stand while she does, so we would not wish to see her go.'

He looked around him. 'This is her place, Chiara, her first and her last. Can't you feel it?'

She'd thought that all her awareness was focused on him, yet as he spoke she realised there was another element in the tense atmosphere—another kind of stillness that did not seem to belong to this world at all, but to some distant, primeval time.

Dry-mouthed, she whispered, 'Yes...'

'Drink some water.' His voice was gentle. He walked forward and took down a small metal cup which stood on a ledge at the statue's feet, holding it under the stream of water. 'It is safe. See?' He drank himself, then passed her the cup. The water was like ice, but she gulped it gratefully, and handed the cup back with a murmured word of thanks.

'Shall we go back to the house?' Guido poured the last few drops of water on the ground, and replaced the cup on its ledge.

'Oh, I thought I'd walk on a little further,' Clare fibbed hastily.

'I do not advise it.'

She stiffened. 'Is that an order, *signore*?'

'No,' he said. 'Merely some advice. At this level you are safe enough, but these are not gentle English woods.

Wild boar have been seen in the locality, and wolves. And you should wear more substantial shoes,' he added, directing a critical glance at her sandals. 'There are snakes too.'

'Oh.' Clare bit her lip. 'In that case, I'll certainly go back.'

'A wise decision,' he said softly. 'Minerva's influence is working already.'

She gave him a mutinous look and started back along the track, keeping a careful eye on the ground for stray vipers.

When they reached the steps, 'Perhaps I should go first,' Guido suggested. 'Sometimes it can be treacherous here if there has been recent heavy rain.'

'It was perfectly safe coming up,' Clare began, and immediately slipped on a loose stone, sliding forward to collide heavily with Guido. She cried out in panic, thinking they were both bound to fall, but it was like hitting Minerva's rockface. He didn't move an inch, apart from the arm that fastened round her like a vice, preventing her from slipping any further.

'Thank you,' she said, when she'd controlled her flurried breathing. She tried to laugh. 'That was stupid of me.'

He did not share her amusement. Nor did he unclamp his arm from round her waist. His face was grave, almost bitter as he looked down at her. 'And I am also a fool,' he said softly, and kissed her.

He was not gentle this time. Nor did he hurry. It was a deliberate, totally sensual ravishment of her mouth, as if, she thought dazedly, he was putting his mark on her for all eternity. He pulled her closer, crushing her breasts against him, as if he intended to absorb her into his physical being, while one muscular leg ruthlessly parted her thighs, pressing on her in blatant erotic demand.

She gasped, her body convulsing in startled pleasure, her head falling back helplessly. But he captured her face between both hands, bringing her swollen mouth back to his, the subtle thrust of his tongue mimicking the more intimate contact that his thigh was enforcing.

His hands left her face, moving slowly down her throat and over her shoulders, in hungry search of her breasts. His fingertips spread the fabric of her shirt, drawing it tight, so that the aroused nipples were clearly visible. For a long moment he stared down at her, then slowly he released the buttons on her shirt, pushing the loosened edges away from her body.

His hands moved on her gently, cupping the soft flesh with exquisite, lingering delicacy. His fingers brushed the hard peaks, sending burning shafts of sensation through her body to her loins.

Then, he bent his head, and she felt the burning moisture of his mouth moving achingly on her naked, eager body.

She was spiralling out of control fast, her hands twisting crazily in his shirt-front, trying to drag it apart so that she could feel his skin bare against hers. A wordless sob was rising in her throat. Sunlight, trees, and the baked stony earth were spinning round her in a dizzying circle.

He lifted his head and looked down at her, his face stark, his breathing hoarse.

He said, '*Dio*, I meant to be patient, I swear it. To wait for you. But I cannot—*cannot. Mia bella*, we must not stay here. Come with me now. Let me make you happy...'

The temptation was unbearable. All she wanted in this

life was to yield—to go wherever he wished to take her—become whatever he wanted.

Only, she realised with heart-numbing suddenness, she would have to live with the consequences for the rest of her life. And that life would be spent alone.

'No.' The word was torn from her, hurting her throat. She dragged herself free, backing away across the path, half collapsing against the trunk of a tree as she struggled to pull her shirt across her breasts. A first step on the way to regain sanity and a modicum of self-respect.

'Chiara.' His voice broke on the word. 'You can't do this to me—to us. I cannot bear it.'

'Us?' she echoed. 'There is no "us".' She invested the tiny word with scorn. 'And you don't have to bear a thing, *signore*. I'm the one who's going to be left feeling used, and worthless.'

'No.' He took a step towards here, hand outstretched pleadingly.

She recoiled. 'Don't come any nearer.'

'I will stay here,' he said. 'I will not move; I swear it. I shall wait for you to come to me.'

'Then you'll wait a long time. Because this is where I belong, Marchese. On the other side of the track. Thank God I remembered in time.'

'*Mia cara.*' Guido drew a deep breath. She saw the muscles move convulsively in his throat. 'Listen to me, I beg of you. You don't understand...'

'But I do,' she said. 'I understand only too well, and I despise myself for getting into this situation. Because it's happened to me before. Isn't that incredible? Isn't that your actual nightmare?' She gave a small, harsh laugh.

'But this time I can step back,' she went on. 'Because

I decided a long time ago that I was never going to be anyone's—piece on the side, Marchese.'

She saw him flinch, his mouth hardening in distaste, and pressed on.

'Oh, I'm sure you could make me forget everything— at least for a while. I don't doubt your technique is second to none. But in the end my conscience—my sense of honour—would be waiting for me. And it's easier to run from you than from them.

'And don't take my rejection too much to heart,' she added. She wanted to hurt him, as she herself was wounded. Wanted to use words against him, as if they were stones she had picked up from the ground and thrown. 'I'm sure you have a waiting list. After all, you're the man who has everything—looks, brains, and all that wonderful money to buy yourself wives and mistresses by the cart-load.

'But you forgot one thing. As I've said before, I'm not for sale.'

'Have you finished?' The harshness in his voice stopped her dead, the breath catching in her throat.

'Yes.' She flung back her head defiantly, when in reality, she wanted to howl like a banshee. 'I hope I've made myself clear.'

His face was a death mask, his eyes like winter. He was no longer the man who'd kissed her into delirium— caressed her to the edge of madness—but a formidable, forbidding stranger. 'Clear as crystal, *signorina*. As a first step, I suggest we take our separate ways back to the house.' He paused. 'And in future I shall ensure that our paths cross as little as possible.'

He turned and walked away, back up to the plateau and out of her sight.

The moan came from deep inside her, filling her head

with its animal keening. She had not believed she was capable of such a sound—or of such pain either.

Uncaring of her safety, she turned and plunged down the steps, gaining momentum with every step.

Suddenly she heard voices, and grabbed at the rope to slow herself, narrowly avoiding crashing into Violetta and the Count, who were preparing to start the ascent.

'*Carissima.*' Violetta's voice was shocked. 'What is the matter? Why are you dashing about like a madwoman?'

'You should not run on these steps, dear child,' the Count added, his face concerned. 'It is not safe. You could break your neck.'

Under the circumstances, Clare thought, as she muttered an incoherent apology, that would be a bonus.

And she began to run again to the villa, leaving them staring after her.

CHAPTER NINE

'THERE.' Paola tossed the glossy magazine she'd been reading from on to the tiles beside her lounger. 'I managed every word. I am so good.'

Clare smiled at her. 'Yes,' she agreed gently. 'You're doing very well.' But only when Paola was translating features about fashion and beauty or high-level gossip, she reminded herself wryly. Faced with anything more intellectual, her pupil went into sulky reverse. And she also insisted that lessons were combined with sunbathing by the pool— 'So that they are not like school.'

'The Marchese will be pleased,' she added with a touch of constraint.

Paola tossed her head. 'Perhaps—but what does it matter? I still shall not marry him.' She shrugged. 'And I do not believe he wishes it any longer, either. After all, he is never here.'

It was no more than the truth, Clare acknowledged with an inward sigh. Since that traumatic parting between them on the track below the Minerva shrine three weeks ago, Guido had been as good as his word.

Their paths had barely crossed at all, because he had spent minimal time at the villa. And she had never again found herself alone with him, even accidentally.

When she did encounter him these days, it was solely on formal occasions in the dining room, or in the *salone* during the evening, and Clare found herself treated with exquisite but chilling politeness.

And no matter how many times she assured herself

141

that it was all for the best—and exactly what she wanted—nothing could dull the pain of longing that drove her early to the silence of her bedroom each night. But not to sleep. That was too much to hope for.

Instead, she lay, staring into the darkness, counting the hours, as the slatted moonlight moved slowly across the floor, her whole body aroused and alive, yearning for the surcease of a fulfilment forever denied.

The celibacy she'd adopted since James's departure from her life had never been a particular burden. She'd embraced it with a kind of relief, telling herself it was the only way to protect herself from betrayal and heartbreak. Because physical passion made you vulnerable.

Now she knew that all she'd experienced with James was the denting of her self-esteem. That she'd never come close to loving him.

She'd learned a hard and bitter way what it was to care in real earnest. To need a man as simply and essentially as she needed to draw breath.

She'd tried in vain to argue with herself that she was confusing lust with love. That what she felt for Guido was sheer infatuation—a brief flame that would flicker and die. More importantly that she hardly knew him for God's sake. In the normal timescale of relationships they were still strangers.

And yet—and yet...

The first time she'd seen him there'd been a kind of recognition. An immediate shock to her senses. The first time he'd touched her some unbridgeable gulf had been leapt.

As if we'd always known, she thought. As if our lives had always been moving towards this moment.

Except that it wasn't true, and hadn't happened. Except in her own too-vivid imagination.

She lashed herself with self-derision. What had passed between Guido and herself was no mating of two souls. He'd made a pass, and she'd stupidly responded, and that was all. Anything further was just a useless attempt to justify her own pathetic foolishness.

Guido Bartaldi was an expert at seduction, and she'd almost allowed herself to be seduced. Nearly, but not quite, and it was his turn to have a bruised ego.

Every time he set eyes on her the memory of her rejection must be at the forefront of his mind, she reflected without pleasure. The cold civility of his manner was an effective barrier to the anger and resentment that she must have provoked.

But how she missed the gleam of laughter in his eyes when he looked at her the teasing note in his voice. The way he said 'Chiara'.

She hadn't realised how much it all meant to her until it was gone, and she couldn't call it back. Couldn't build on that laughter, and the way his voice caressed her.

She mourned for them almost more than his kisses. Almost...

She said quietly now, 'I don't think there's been any change of plan, Paola. He's a busy man, that's all.' She paused. 'When he is here, he's—attentive, isn't he?'

She knew the answer to that, because she saw it happening. Guido Bartaldi's wooing of his future wife was lightly and charmingly done. If he was away for more than two days at a time, there was invariably a gift— some expensive trifle. But, physically, he was imposing no pressure at all, and that was clever, Clare admitted with a pang.

Because, in spite of her protests, Paola was bound to be just a little intrigued, and would soon start to wonder precisely why he did not try to make love to her.

And, once he did make his claim, Clare could not believe that Paola would be able to maintain her resistance for any length of time. Not, she thought unhappily, when she was being manipulated by an expert.

She could only hope she'd be long gone by that time. Because she could not bear to watch him coax Paola to surrender. Or any other woman, for that matter.

'He is generous.' Paola shrugged again. She sent Clare a sly sideways look. 'So that I will not guess how much time he spends in Siena. My stepmother says that a man who gives so many presents has a guilty conscience.'

'And the renovation of the chapel for the wedding?' Clare queried coolly, as pain twisted inside her. 'Is that a sign of guilt too?'

Paola looked mutinous. 'Guido is not doing that for me. It is part of his precious house, and must be protected.'

'Like the Minerva shrine,' Clare said half to herself.

Paola gave her a surprised look. 'You have seen that?'

Clare bent to put the magazines together and disguise the faint colour that had risen to her face. 'Why, yes, when I first arrived. I went for a walk and—found it.'

'I am surprised Guido allowed it, that is all.' Paola's tone was dismissive. 'Usually he does not permit those outside the family to venture so far. The statue is very old and valuable, as well as ugly, and there are many stories about it—legends.' She pulled a face. 'I do not understand the fuss.'

'It's precisely because the statue is very old and valuable,' Clare said drily. 'And I think it's beautiful. It gives off this—aura of quiet and peace.'

She knew by the expression on Paola's face that she might as well have been speaking Mandarin Chinese.

'Anyway,' the younger girl continued after a pause,

'Guido would not have his wedding hidden away here, when it happens—if it happens—it will be in Rome, and his great-uncle the cardinal will perform the ceremony.'

'Is that what you would prefer?'

'I?' Paola asked. 'I shall not be there.'

She swung her legs to the floor, and began to collect her things together. 'I am going back to the house now. I have a headache.'

'Another one?' Clare raised her eyebrows. 'That's the third this week, Paola. Maybe you should see a doctor.'

'I do not need a doctor.' Her tone was pettish. 'Just a rest from all this stupid translation. I will see you at dinner, if my head is better. *Ciao.*'

Clare sighed, and lay back on her own lounger. Paola's acquaintance with English was improving daily, but the same could not be said about her attitude towards her proposed marriage.

And Clare had tried. Each day she tried to sell Paola the charms of the Villa Minerva and its environs, together with the potent advantages of being a rich Marchesa, but the other girl still wasn't buying.

'This place is like a graveyard,' was her usual reply. 'And I do not need to marry a rich man. I shall have money of my own.' Stalemate.

I can teach, Clare thought, biting her lip. But I'm not so hot on persuasion. But then my heart's not in it. I'm on her side. I don't think this wedding should take place either, and for more than just selfish reasons.

On the brighter side, at least Paola was not rhapsodising about Fabio with every breath. In fact she didn't mention him at all, which Clare could only be thankful for. Maybe he'd decided that Paola was too well guarded, and had faded out of the picture.

However, that did not mean that Paola would turn to

Guido for comfort—especially as he was openly pursuing his own interests, she thought unhappily. And that after she'd warned him that Paola knew about his Sienese lady.

She heard someone coming down the steps leading to the pool and looked round, smiling, as Tonio Lerucci came into view.

'Did I wake you? I'm sorry.' He gave her his swift, wide smile. 'I thought Paola was here.'

'I wasn't asleep.' Clare sat up. 'And Paola's gone back to the house to rest. I think she's feeling the heat.'

He nodded, fanning himself with his hand as he sat down on the vacant lounger. 'I think the weather will break soon. There are storms forecast.'

'The air feels heavy enough,' Clare agreed. Perhaps Paola's headache was genuine, she thought, lifting her hair away from the nape of her neck.

Tonio was speaking. 'I came to ask if she wanted another tennis lesson this evening before dinner. When it is cooler.'

'I'll ask her for you when I go up to the house.' Clare smiled back at him. 'You're a miracle worker, getting her to play. I thought she loathed sport.'

'No,' he said. 'When she was a child, she was very good—very athletic. It is her stepmother in Rome who has persuaded her that it isn't cool to exert herself.' There was a certain bitterness in his voice. 'That she should lie about all day long and live a useless life.'

Clare said slowly, 'Of course, you've known her a long time, haven't you?'

'Yes.' There was an odd bleakness in his voice that alerted her suddenly. 'But sometimes she seems to forget that.'

Clare bit her lip. 'I don't think she's in a very easy

position. She sees her life being mapped out for her, and she hasn't been consulted on the route. And she doesn't like it here.'

'She used to.' There was a wealth of sadness in his voice. 'I thought she could be happy here again. But now I'm not so sure.'

'I think,' Clare said, picking her way carefully, 'that marrying the right man would make a difference.'

Tonio spread his hands. He said with a touch of harshness, 'Then there is no problem. All she has to do is agree, and the wedding could take place tomorrow.'

She said, 'Unfortunately, it isn't that simple, and I think you know that. Because she isn't convinced that he is right for her.' She swallowed. 'It would help if Guido—if the Marchese—spent less time—away. In Siena and other places,' she added constrainedly.

He shook his head. 'At the moment he has no choice. The boutique chain is taking off, and he likes to supervise the details himself.'

'Oh,' she said. 'And is that all he's doing? Hasn't he other more personal reasons for being there?'

Tonio looked uncomfortable. He said, 'Forgive me, this is not something I can discuss. It is Guido's private business.'

'But no secret,' she said. 'As Paola knows all about it.'

'No,' he said quietly. 'She does not. No one does, except the Marchese himself.'

'You condone what he's doing?'

'It is not my place to judge.' He paused. 'Or to explain. Guido does what he must, he always has.'

'You're very loyal.'

He bent his head. 'As he is himself. As you will realise one day.' He smiled awkwardly and rose to his feet.

'If you would be kind enough to pass my message to Paola?'

Clare was thoughtful as she walked up to the house. She had seen a good deal of Tonio over the past weeks, and liked him more at each encounter. And he had infinite patience with Paola, she reflected ruefully, even when she was at her worst. Nothing she did seemed to faze him.

At the same time, she was a little surprised that Guido should allow him to spend so much time in Paola's company. Apart from the tennis, on most days he came down to the pool to encourage her to swim. And in the evenings he was teaching her backgammon, and dancing with her when there was music after dinner in the *salone*.

Perhaps he was just ensuring that she didn't become bored—and rebellious again.

But Guido should be doing that, she thought. Not appointing a deputy, however faithful and discreet.

She knocked softly at Paola's door on the way to her own room and called her name, but there was no answer. Probably she'd taken some painkillers and gone to sleep, she decided as she turned away.

The long shutters had been closed over the window in her room, and she walked across, pushing them ajar to admit some light. Below her the gardens shimmered in the intense sunlight.

Clare shaded her eyes, and stared at the wooded slopes in the distance. She thought longingly of Minerva, standing in her rocky niche, with the torrent of icy water falling past her. She'd made several pilgrimages to the shrine over the past weeks, always when Guido was away. And always she'd had the place entirely to herself.

She'd sat on the grass going over and over in her mind

everything that had transpired between Guido and herself. Trying to see if there was anything she could have done to change things.

And having to accept that there was not. Because she and Guido wanted totally different things from their relationships. She needed commitment, whereas he would have settled for transience. She wanted fidelity, but for him variety was the name of the game. For her marriage was about love. For him it involved convenience—a merging of money and interests.

And it was better by far to end it as she had done than to risk ultimate heartbreak.

She moved her shoulders under the damp cling of her top. Guido was away today, and there was nothing to prevent her making the climb up to the shrine—except the heat.

But some brave soul was risking it, she realised, as she sighted a flash of bright yellow moving among the trees.

Clare frowned. 'Who on earth?' she said aloud.

It couldn't be Violetta, because she'd gone with the Count to have lunch with some friends in Gubbio and had not yet returned.

But Paola has a dress that colour, she thought restively. The same Paola who feels the heat so badly, and is allegedly flaked out on her bed at this moment.

So why do I know, without checking, that I won't find her there?

She groaned inwardly. Part of her was tempted to let Paola go to the devil in her own way. But she knew in her heart that she had to intervene—to find out what was going on. Because that was what she was being paid for.

She was in no good mood when she reached the gate in the wall and wrenched it open. The sun was beating down on her, and her clothes were sticking to her body. She had to force her legs up the steps, the rope rasping on her damp hand.

When she reached the place where the track divided, she paused, listening intently, but there was no sound except the distant rush of water.

She found Paola standing in front of the shrine, staring up at the statue. She was surprised to see that she was alone—and that she appeared to have been crying.

The angry demand for an explanation died unuttered. Instead, she said gently, 'Paola? Is something wrong? What are you doing here?'

'You come here.' The other's voice was husky. 'You said it was peaceful. Perhaps I too wish to be quiet sometimes. To think.'

Clare bit her lip. 'Then I'm sorry I intruded,' she returned. 'I'll leave you to it.'

'No—wait. I wish to ask you something.' Paola paused. 'Chiara, is it possible to think that you are in love with someone, and suddenly realise it is not true. That you really care for someone else entirely—and have done for a long time—only you have been too blind, too stubborn to admit it? Can that happen?'

Clare was very still. 'Yes,' she said slowly. 'I'd say that could happen quite easily.'

Paola sighed. 'I was afraid of that.' She was silent for a moment. 'Chiara—I have been seeing Fabio. He has been here at the villa, pretending to be a gardener.'

Clare closed her eyes for a moment. 'My God,' she said. 'Marco's cousin.'

'You knew it was him?'

'Not till now, but I should have done. I knew there was something wrong about him.'

Paola nodded. '*Si*, there was something wrong. He

wanted money—only money. At first, he talked of love—how happy we would be. But then he began to change—to plan how to get money from Guido. To ask all the time about my inheritance. And I began to see that was all that mattered to him.

'At the same time, I realised who I truly loved, even though I have fought against it for so long. And I saw that he is the only man who could make me happy. So today, when I met Fabio, I told him that it was all over—finished.'

'And how did he react?'

'He was angry. He said I had made a fool of him, and that he would make me sorry for it. And make Guido sorry, too.' Her eyes met Clare's apprehensively. 'Do you think he can.'

'No,' Clare denied robustly. She swallowed past the sudden tightness in her throat. 'But if you're worried— talk to Guido about it.'

'I cannot.' Paola shook her head. 'Not when there is so much else that I must say to him. So much I must explain, and ask him to forgive.'

Clare smiled tautly. 'I don't think that will be a problem. I'm sure he'll meet you more than halfway.'

There were tears in Paola's eyes again. 'Oh, you are good to me, Chiara. It was you who first made me doubt Fabio, although I did not wish to.' She took Clare's hand. 'You will stay, won't you, for my wedding?'

'I'll try, but it may be difficult,' Clare said huskily. 'I will need to find another job.' She paused. 'Paola—you are sure—you want this marriage...?'

'Si.' Paola smiled almost shyly. 'I feel as if I have come home. Can you understand that?'

'Yes,' Clare said. 'I understand perfectly.'

*   *   *

Guido returned to the villa just before dinner that evening. Clare did not see his arrival, but she was aware of it all the same. There was always a new vibrancy in the air when Guido was at home. A tingle in the atmosphere which echoed in her bloodstream, making her heart beat faster.

She stood, looking at herself in the mirror. Tonight would be a time for celebration, so she'd put on the dress that Violetta had bought her in Perugia. It seemed a tiny bit looser than it had done, signalling that she'd lost some weight. Her cheekbones were more pronounced too, she thought critically, and there were tense lines along her jaw and throat.

Everything was combining to betray her inner turmoil, she thought unhappily. But, hopefully, no one would be looking at her. All attention would be turned to Guido and Paola.

She told herself that she should be glad for them. Relieved that Paola had been saved from making a terrible mistake with Fabio. And there was no doubt that she would be pampered and protected for the rest of her life as the Marchesa Bartaldi. But was that enough? Wouldn't she want to love and be loved in equal proportion? Could Guido's indulgence ever be enough?

She shook her head. She must stop thinking like this. It would soon be none of her concern, anyway. Her job was done and she could hand in her notice.

But first she had to get through this evening, which promised to be the most difficult of her life.

She went slowly downstairs, and stood, hesitating, listening to the voices coming from the *salone*. The excitement in the air was almost tangible.

She saw that Guido's study door was standing open, and drew a deep breath. There would never be a better time to tell him she was leaving. The way things stood between them, he could only be relieved to see the back of her.

She reached the doorway, and peeped into the room. Guido was there, but not alone. Paola was with him, in his arms, her face buried against his shoulder while his hand stroked her hair with unmistakable tenderness.

As Clare stood motionless, lips parted and eyes enormous, he lifted his head sharply and looked at her, and she saw his face, grim, almost haggard, his mouth set, his whole expression at total variance with the gentleness of his embrace.

For a long moment they were locked together, in a kind of shocked, bitter awareness, his dark gaze sweeping her, burning her.

Until with a small sound between a sob and an apology, Clare turned and sped away.

CHAPTER TEN

'DEAR child.' Violetta's voice was full of concern. 'You look ill. What has happened?'

Clare forced a travesty of a smile. 'I have this splitting headache. There must be a storm coming. Thunder always affects me like this.' She hesitated. 'I was wondering if you had your painkillers with you.'

'But of course.' Violetta produced her leather vanity case. 'They are in here, *cara*. Also tissues, and a bottle of my special cologne. Take whatever you need.' She paused. 'Is there anything else I can get you? Matteo says you are not coming down to dinner. May he bring you a light supper on a tray, perhaps? Some soup and fruit?'

'No—no, thank you.' Clare bit her lip. 'I'm really not hungry.'

'Such a shame.' Violetta patted her cheek gently. 'When there is to be a celebration. And you look so beautiful in that dress, although pale. Paola has told you her news, of course? Such happiness.'

'Yes,' Clare said steadily. 'Such happiness.'

I meant to be brave, she thought, as she stood at the window in her room, staring rigidly and sightlessly down at the garden, held in the heavy hush of evening. But that was before I saw them together. Before I saw her in his arms. And knew I couldn't bear it.

She'd exaggerated her headache, of course, to avoid having to present herself downstairs, but there was a dull throb above her eyes, and a bitter, shaking emptiness inside her just the same.

She had promised Violetta she would take the capsules and go straight to bed, but she didn't seem capable even of that small amount of effort.

When the door behind her suddenly opened, she presumed her godmother was coming to check on her.

She said, wearily, 'Please don't bully me, Violetta. I'm going to bed right now.'

'It is not the Signora.' Guido's voice was harsh, almost inimical.

She spun round with a gasp, watching in shock as he kicked the door shut behind him.

'What are you doing here?'

'I am being a good host,' he said coldly. 'Asking after the health of one of my guests. A guest, it seems, who prefers sheltering behind minor illnesses to confronting life.'

Angry colour flooded her face. 'That's not fair. And I've had more than my share of confrontation since we met, Marchese.'

'You sought me out earlier,' he said. 'What did you want?'

'To give you formal notice.' Her heart was hammering, her breath rasping in her chest. 'To tell you that I was leaving.'

'It is more usual to put such a communication in writing,' Guido said curtly. 'In any event, you are wasting your time. I shall not accept your notice.'

'My job here has finished,' she said huskily. 'You have no reason—no right to detain me any longer.'

'Do not speak to me of rights.' He flung back his head. His eyes blazed at her. 'This is my house, Chiara. This is my land. And I am Bartaldi. I exercise what rights I choose. As for reasons—you know as well as I do why I wish you to remain.'

'You wish—*you wish.*' She threw the words at him. 'And what about my wishes—my feelings? What if I say I can't bear to stay under the same roof with you a moment longer?'

'Tell what lie you please. It makes no difference. There is no escape.' Hands on hips he regarded her, his mouth twisting sardonically. 'I have seen your eyes follow me these last three weeks, as mine have followed you. The shadows in your face tell me you have shared my sleepless nights. Until you share my bed, Chiara, I doubt I shall ever sleep again.'

'Then enjoy your insomnia,' she said fiercely. 'For God's sake, *signore*, how many women do you want in your life?'

'I need only one, Chiara. I need you.' He took a step towards her. His voice deepened, gentled. 'You are tearing me in pieces, *mia bella.*'

She said hoarsely, 'Don't come near me. Don't say these things. You're cruel, *signore*. Cruel.'

'Then let us be kind to each other, *carissima.*' A small laugh forced itself from his throat. 'Let us comfort each other for the misery of the last three weeks.'

'And what about the wretchedness of the rest of our lives? How do we deal with that?' She lifted her chin. 'Oh, I forgot. You have your lady in Siena.'

His mouth tightened. 'Yes,' he said. 'And no doubt she would give me kindness, if I asked her. Only I shall not do so. I cannot, and one day you will understand why.'

She shook her head. 'I don't think so. I don't think I'll ever understand anything that's happened in these past weeks. All I know is that I wish I was a thousand miles away—and that I'd never set eyes on you.' Her voice broke on a little wail of pure misery.

'Go away, Guido, please. Go back where you belong—to the people you belong to. And leave me in peace.'

'Peace.' He laughed harshly. 'I doubt, *mia bella* if you and I will ever know peace again. And, unlike you, if I could stretch out this moment when you fill my eyes through all eternity, I would do it. I—do not think you know how beautiful you are.'

Clare saw a muscle move convulsively in his throat.

'But if you hate the sight of me so much, there is an easy remedy,' he went on, his voice low and bitter. 'Just close your eyes, and I will be gone from you. Do it, Chiara. Do it now.'

Almost helplessly, she obeyed. As the blank darkness surrounded her, she was suddenly, poignantly aware of his nearness, then the touch of his lips on her hair, her forehead, and her closed lids.

'*Adio,*' he whispered. 'My sweet one. My beloved.'

Then there was nothing, and she knew that she was alone.

And more lonely than she had ever been in her life.

When she could think coherently again, and make her paralysed muscles obey her, she found herself reaching for Violetta's vanity case, fumbling through its contents for the promised painkillers. As if there was any panacea for the agony that was tearing her apart.

I shouldn't feel like this, she told herself desperately. Because he isn't worth it. He's just another love cheat, going into marriage for cynical commercial reasons with no intention of being faithful. I ought to hate him. I *want* to hate him. But I can't, and I despise myself for it.

Oh, where were those capsules? Her unshed tears were like an iron band tightening behind her eyes. She up-ended the case on the bed, and Violetta's car keys fell with a clunk on to the floor at her feet.

She bent, slowly, and retrieved them. Held them in her hand.

Guido had said there was no escape. But here was Fate intervening, and showing her a way out.

And she had to take it. Because the simple truth was she did not trust herself to stay another hour where Guido was. And certainly not another night.

She shivered, her fingers closing round the keys, digging them into her soft palm.

She would drive to the nearest station, she thought feverishly. Catch a train to—anywhere. Cover her tracks so well that even Guido's power could not follow her.

Do what she should have done weeks ago. He'd thwarted her then. Now he would not get the chance.

She couldn't risk taking all her things. Her leather shoulder bag was capacious enough to accommodate a change of underwear and a few essential toiletries, as well as her passport and money. So that would have to do.

Besides, if—anyone came searching for her, clothes left hanging in the wardrobe would give the impression that her absence was a temporary one. That she'd gone out for an evening stroll, perhaps. Which would give her some precious leeway.

She needed to change now, of course. She rifled along the hanging rail and dragged out a chocolate-coloured shift, and a hip-length cream jacket. She couldn't afford to look too casual.

As she turned away to unzip her dress, she caught a glimpse of herself in the mirror, and saw what he had seen. A girl, her blonde hair dishevelled, her dark eyes wide and brilliant, and faint colour emphasising her cheekbones. The black dress hinted discreetly at the slender curves it concealed, down to the deep slash in the skirt, which showed off one slim, black-stockinged leg.

'Beautiful,' she whispered, as tears stung her eyes and the image suddenly blurred. 'He said I looked beautiful.'

She shook her head impatiently. There would be time enough to cry. Now she had to concentrate on her get-away.

She was half afraid Guido might have forestalled her by appointing one of the servants to wait outside her door, but the gallery and stairs were deserted. Judging by the hum of voices, they were all now in the dining room. And her quickest route to where Violetta's car was parked would take her straight past the windows.

I can't risk it, she told herself. I'll go the long way round. Circle the house.

She made herself walk steadily, looking appreciatively around her at the twilit garden. Just as if she was taking an evening stroll.

Her steps slowed when she reached the chapel. There was scaffolding round it, and the damaged window had already been replaced.

An artist in stained glass from Florence had done the work, and it was magnificent, Violetta had enthused to her.

'You must go to look at it, *mia cara*.'

She'd nodded, and smiled, and known she would do no such thing. She didn't want to see the place where Guido and Paola would be married restored to its former glory. Unless, of course, the wedding took place in Rome after all.

The *campanile* was still out of bounds, however, while its damage was being assessed, but there was real doubt over whether or not it could be saved.

It had been a graceful, pretty building before the earthquake. Now its bell had fallen, and its top stones lay in rubble around the base.

It was securely boarded up, and as Clare went past she was surprised to see that some of the planks had been torn down, and were propped against the wall.

She was even more astonished to see a car parked at the side of it.

Maybe the architect had returned for another survey, she thought. But surely he wouldn't choose to do so in the half-light. Unless, of course, Guido had invited him up to the villa for dinner.

But the car didn't look as if it belonged to a successful professional man. It was too elderly and battered.

Frowning, Clare walked over for a closer look. As she reached the driver's side and looked through the window she heard the sound of voices, and instinctively ducked down, peeping across the bonnet.

Two men came out of the *campanile*, carrying something between them. Something heavy, trussed up in sacking and rope.

For a moment she thought it was a body, and clapped a hand over her mouth to prevent a scream.

'Careful, you fool.' Although Clare had only met the speaker once, his voice was instantly familiar.

My God, she thought. It's Fabio.

'If you break it, you've lost us a fortune,' he went on impatiently.

They opened the boot and lowered their burden into it, muttering and cursing.

Clare stayed where she was. She'd no idea what they

were doing, but she'd no wish to be caught watching them do it.

After a whispered interchange, they went back into the *campanile* and Clare straightened. They were clearly up to no good, and she knew she should report them. But going back to the house would give herself away too. And besides, her priority was reaching Violetta's car.

I'll stop at the first public phone, she promised herself, treading carefully to the back of the car and bracing herself for a swift sprint round the corner of the villa to safety.

The boot was open, and she was unable to resist a swift sideways glance. And froze. Some of the sacking had fallen away to reveal the calm stone face of the Minerva.

The statue, she thought, suddenly frantic. They're stealing the statue.

'Good evening, *signorina*.' Fabio's voice spoke behind her, and she whirled round with a cry. 'I thought it was you, scrabbling in the dust. Not very dignified for Bartaldi's woman.'

She said, 'Don't you dare to speak to me like that. And what are you doing with the Minerva?'

'Oh, we're just going to keep it safe while your Marchese decides how much it is worth to him. Paola showed me where it was, and told me the legend. If the statue falls, the house of Bartaldi falls with it.' He smiled unpleasantly. 'I wonder just how superstitious the Marchese will prove to be?'

'I thought you'd already learned that he doesn't respond to ransom demands.' Clare's tone was terse.

'Ah,' he said. 'But a piece of stone doesn't talk too much, or leave letters lying about that it shouldn't.

Paola's more trouble than she's worth, but I should end up making more money than I ever dreamed of.'

'You'll never get away with it.'

'No?' His smile widened. 'And who's going to tell on us. You, *signorina*? I don't think so. Because you're going to be the icing on a very large cake. I think Bartaldi will pay handsomely to get you back, *ragazza*.'

He looked past her and nodded, and Clare found herself suddenly enveloped in a blanket, thrown over her from the rear. She kicked and struggled and tried to scream, but the cloth, old and musty, muffled the sound. Meanwhile a cord was being wound round her, pinning her wrists to her body. Still kicking, she was picked up bodily and thrown into the car.

For a moment she was winded, and lay gasping.

'Not as soft as Bartaldi's bed, eh, pretty one?' Fabio's voice was gloating and hateful. 'Don't worry. You'll soon be back in it, once your lover hands over the money.'

She tried to cry out, to tell them they were crazy, that Guido wouldn't pay one solitary lira for her, but the car engine started with a sullen roar, drowning her words.

It was a bumpy, jolting ride, and it seemed to last an eternity. Clare lay still, trying to gulp air through the holes in the blanket and avoid being thrown off the seat at the same time. She was also trying to work out in time and distance how far they travelled, but it was impossible. Being cocooned like this made her totally disoriented.

To her own surprise, she felt angry rather than scared. She remembered Guido had not considered Fabio dangerous, just lazy and greedy. On the look-out for easy money.

But, by stealing the Minerva, he might have bitten off more than he could chew.

She remembered hearing somewhere that if you flexed and relaxed your muscles when you were tied up, the rope became looser, but she'd been tied up like a parcel. The rope bit into her arms and body. She was just becoming seriously uncomfortable when, at last, the car stopped with a squeal of brakes. Wherever they were, Fabio obviously wasn't concerned about being heard.

She heard the car door open, behind her, then she was being tugged out ignominiously.

'Stand, *raggazza*,' she was ordered. 'Now walk forward.'

They were on each side of her. She gauged their proximity, then kicked out as hard as she could, screaming loudly at the same time.

She connected with them both, gasps of pain rewarding her, and for a moment the hands holding her slackened their grip. She tried to run, then something struck her on the head, and the darkness inside the blanket became swirling and dense, and she fell forward into it.

Her eyelids seemed to have been glued down, and opening them was a lengthy and burdensome chore.

When she managed it, she found herself looking up at the dim light coming from a low-watt bulb guarded by a fluted floral shade.

Not a cellar, then, she thought, lifting her aching head and looking round. Nor her idea of a kidnappers' den— if she'd ever had one.

In fact, her prison screamed suburban bedroom. She was lying on a single bed on a thickly woven white bedspread, and she saw that her sandals had been removed, presumably to protect the pristine surface.

I'm glad my captors remembered their manners, she thought ironically.

But she was still very much a prisoner. Her feet were free, but her hands were tightly secured behind her back.

She went on looking round. The floor was polished wood, with a few rugs scattered about, and there were one or two pieces of old-fashioned, highly-polished furniture.

Behind the floral curtains were heavy shutters, which common sense told her would be securely locked.

So now what? She wondered, relapsing gingerly back on to her pillow. She didn't even know what time it was, and, even if she twisted herself in half, she couldn't see her wristwatch.

So, all she could do was wait.

But she didn't have to wait long. She heard the sound of a key in the lock, and a young man, presumably her other assailant, came in. He was shorter than Fabio, and stockily built, with a broad face which, she thought, would usually have been good-humoured, but now looked sullenly apprehensive.

'So you are awake.' There was a note of relief in his voice which didn't escape her. Clearly they'd worked out that causing her physical damage was not to their advantage. 'How do you feel?'

'Never better,' Clare returned with heavy irony. She looked at the strong hands with their callused palms and made a deduction. 'You must be Marco.'

He flushed, giving her a scared, resentful look. 'How did you know that?'

'Because you look as if you spend your life out of doors—unlike your friend.' She paused. 'Will you untie me, please?'

'No, that I cannot do, *signorina*.'

'Well, you'll have to do so eventually,' Clare said crisply. 'I need the bathroom.'

He went out, muttering, and returned with Fabio. Together they manoeuvred Clare off the bed, and stood her upright. She was taken out of the room, along a narrow passage, again dimly lit, and decorated with a series of highly coloured holy pictures, to a tiny bathroom, which was really a tiled shower cubicle with extra appointments, including a bidet.

And someone's pride and joy, Clare thought, seeing how it all gleamed with cleanliness.

'No tricks,' Fabio warned as he untied her wrists, and pushed her forward, thrusting a thin, rather hard linen towel at her.

There was one tiny window, high up, so, unless she was Houdini, it was difficult to see what tricks she could get up to, Clare thought ruefully.

She made herself comfortable, then bathed her face and hands with cold water. She looked like hell, she thought, viewing herself critically in the small mirror. She was as pale as death, and there was a bruise on her forehead that was developing into a lump.

But common sense told her she'd probably got off lightly.

'Hurry up.' Fabio banged on the door.

'I need my bag,' she called back. 'What have you done with it?'

'We have it. And we are keeping it. Do you take us for fools?'

'I'd better not answer that,' Clare returned with assumed coolness. 'Just let me have my cosmetic purse, then, and my comb. I'm hardly going to tunnel my way out with my lipstick.'

There was some more muttering, then the door opened and the required items were pushed at her.

Combing her hair, renewing powder and lipstick and spraying herself swiftly with scent wasn't any real help with her problems, but it gave her a psychological boost, which was invaluable.

When she emerged into the passage, she gave them an icy glance. 'And before you tie me up again, I want a glass of water, and something to eat.'

To her surprise, she got both. Marco brought her a bottle of mineral water and a bowl of savoury bean soup. The tray, she saw, had been clumsily laid with a cloth, and there was an elderly starched napkin too.

He stood, shoulders propped against the door, as she ate and drank.

'That was delicious.' She smiled at him when she had finished. He reddened, and muttered something defensive.

'Tell me.' Clare put the napkin on the tray. 'Is Fabio really your cousin?'

He shook his head vehemently. 'No, we met in a bar. He told me he was in love with Signorina Paola, and that the Marchese was keeping them apart.'

'Like Romeo and Juliet?' Clare suggested.

He nodded. '*Si, signorina.* My mother is from Verona, and she has told me that story many times. I felt sorry for Fabio, and he said he would pay me when he and the *signorina* were married. I got him a job on the estate, so that they could meet.'

He hunched his shoulders. 'Only Signor Lerucci sent for me, and told me that he knew I had no cousin, and I have lost my job.' He sent her a sullen look. 'My father worked for the Bartaldi, and his father before him, so this is a great shame for me. When she returns from my sister's house, my mother will be very angry.'

He paused. 'And then Signorina Paola told Fabio that she would not run away with him, so it was all for nothing.' He sighed heavily.

'But Fabio came up with an alternative plan for making money by stealing the Minerva statue?' Clare suggested.

'*Si*. We all know that the Marchese sets great store by the statue. It is an ancient treasure, and very valuable. And Fabio swore to me he would not damage it.'

'And that makes everything all right?' Clare asked. 'I don't think so, Marco.'

'Fabio promised me money,' he insisted. 'Now I have no job, and my mother is not well. And who will employ me when they know I have been dismissed by the Bartaldi? No one.' He sounded very young, suddenly.

A germ of an idea came to Clare. Her lips were parting to speak when the door opened, and Fabio came in carrying the cord for her wrists.

'Is that really necessary?' she asked with distaste.

He grinned at her. 'I think so. You are a valuable property, *signorina*, and you have the advantage that you are made of flesh and blood, not stone. I need to keep you here.'

'Perhaps I'm not worth as much as you think.' Clare lifted her chin. 'The Marchese Bartaldi doesn't respond to blackmail. And he certainly won't be interested in buying me back. I mean nothing to him.'

Fabio's smile widened unpleasantly. 'Good try, *signorina*. Unfortunately, I know differently. Because I saw you together, near the Minerva shrine one afternoon when I had been meeting Paola. And it looked to me as if you meant a great deal.'

He looked her over, making her feel as if she was
coated with slime. 'You are very pretty under your
clothes, *signorina*. Maybe I should get a camera, and
persuade you to undress for me—just to remind the no-
ble Bartaldi what he is missing.'

'Don't be a fool,' Marco broke in, his voice alarmed.
'*Dio*, do not make him angrier than he is already by
shaming his woman. You do not know him. You do not
know what he might do.'

Fabio shrugged. 'Maybe. We will see how generous
his first offer is.' He looked back at Clare, who slowly
released her painful, indrawn breath. 'You will have to
be patient, *signorina*. We have decided to let your lover
stew for a day or two before we make contact. I think
when I talk to him, he will be glad to meet my terms.'

'I wouldn't count on it,' Clare said glacially, as he
retied her wrists.

She kept her head high until they left the room, then
she collapsed on to the edge of the bed, her legs shaking.

The thought that they'd been spied on as Guido
brought her to the edge of surrender made her feel nau-
seous. Her skin crawled at the very idea. She would
never convince Fabio that she wasn't Guido's mistress,
she realised.

But Marco might be a different matter. He was clearly
uneasy about the situation, and that was what she would
work on.

She wondered how soon it would be before she was
missed. In retrospect, leaving her clothes behind didn't
seem such a good idea after all.

Wearily, she swung her legs on to the bed, and made
herself as comfortable as possible. Whatever happened,
going without sleep would solve nothing.

Oh, Guido, she thought as she closed her eyes. Please

come to me. Please find me. And, if you want, I'll stay with you. I'll do anything—be anything you ask.

And for a brief, sweet moment, she imagined she could feel the brush of his lips against her skin, her hair, and her eyelids. And was comforted.

one 'to me. Please find that Jack, if you would. I must warn you, I'd do anything ...' The explicit threat

And for a brief moment before she smothered it, Clare could read the torment in his amber eyes. 'I'll not hurt and her eyelids ...

CHAPTER ELEVEN

WHEN Clare woke, her watch, that she'd removed the previous night, told her it was morning.

She slid awkwardly off the bed, and managed to make her way to the door, turning her back to knock at its panels.

As she'd hoped, Marco appeared, looking no happier than he had the night before.

'*Buongiorno.*' Clare smiled calmly at him. 'I'd like the bathroom, and then some coffee.'

He hesitated, then nodded reluctantly.

As she washed and cleaned her teeth, Clare heard him go downstairs. Scooping her toilet things back into their bag, she opened the door and peeped out.

The passage was empty, and she was sorely tempted to make a dash for it. Except, she reminded herself, that she hadn't a clue where 'it' might be.

A familiar sound was coming from a room across the passage, and she trod softly across and pushed open the door, wrinkling her nose at the smell of grappa which assaulted her. Fabio was sprawled across the bed, an empty bottle on the floor beside him, snoring loudly.

Out for the count, she thought. And the perfect opportunity to work on Marco.

The shutters were open, and she tiptoed across and looked out of the window. As she'd feared, all she could see were fields and trees.

The house, which she was certain belonged to Marco's mother, was in total isolation.

But directly below her was Fabio's car, looking rustier than ever in the sunlight.

If I could just get the keys, she thought. We can't be that far from a main road.

Fabio snorted, and turned on to his side. She crept back to the bathroom, closing the door quietly just as Marco came upstairs with her coffee. In addition, there was a plate, with a slice of ham, a piece of cheese, and a sad-looking peach.

'Thank you.' She sent him another smile. 'How well you look after me. Your mother must be proud of you.' She glanced round her. 'How beautifully she keeps her house.'

'*Grazie, signorina.*' He looked faintly gratified.

'And what a shame she won't be able to stay here,' Clare went on, watching him from under her lashes as she sipped her coffee.

His brow creased. 'What do you mean?'

'Well, she won't be able to look after her house when she's in jail.'

'Jail?' He gave her a stony look. 'My mother will not go to jail. And nor will I. There are many places I can hide—even from Bartaldi.'

'But you've kept me in her house, which will make her an accomplice. At least that's how the police will see it.'

'But you know differently, *signorina*. You will speak for her. She is not young, and she has been sick.'

'Maybe you should have thought about that before you let Fabio involve you in his get-rich schemes,' Clare said contemptuously. She leaned forward, fixing his gaze with hers. She said urgently, 'There is only one person who can speak for you—get you off the hook—and that's the Marchese. And why should he? You betrayed his trust, and now you've stolen from him. You can run, Marco, but he'll hunt you down. And your mother will suffer too.'

'No, that cannot be. Fabio said nothing…'

'Well, why should he? It won't be his mother who'll be arrested. And I'm sure he isn't as caring a son as you, anyway.' Clare shook her head. 'There's no help for it, I'm afraid. When the police trace you to this house, as they will, my fingerprints will be everywhere. And your mother will be involved, up to her neck.'

Marco looked as if he was going to burst into tears. 'I cannot let this happen. What can I do, *signorina*?'

'We-ell.' Clare hesitated, then plunged recklessly. 'You could always let me go.'

'Let you go?' He laughed hoarsely. 'To bring the police down on me and put me in jail? I am not a fool.'

'But it doesn't have to be that way,' Clare said intensely. 'Listen to me, Marco. If you help me get away, I'll tell the Marchese exactly what you did. How kind you've been. How you looked after me. What's more, I'll remind him how long your family have worked for him. I'll even ask for your job back. And there might be a reward,' she added, mentally crossing her fingers.

'He's a good man—a fair man,' she went on quickly. 'He'll forgive you—take you back—if I ask him. If you help me now. And you'll have saved yourself and your mother.'

There was a long silence. Then, 'But how do I know he will do these things?'

Clare lifted her chin. 'Because you have my promise,' she said. 'Because, as Fabio said, I am Bartaldi's woman.'

There was another tense silence. She saw him swallow. Then, 'What do I have to do?'

She couldn't let him see how relieved she was. Instead she tried to sound brisk and matter-of-fact. 'I'm going to need the car. Does Fabio have the keys?'

He nodded. 'He might wake...'

'Only if there's a missile attack.'

'But I am not staying here. I am coming with you, *signorina*. When he does wake, he will be like a crazy man, and I do not want to be here.'

She couldn't blame him, but she needed him like a hole in the head. She supposed he wanted to be sure she would keep her word.

She nodded. 'Whatever you say, Marco. Get the keys and my bag, and we're out of here.'

She watched him go into the room where Fabio was still snoring. After a minute, he reappeared. '*Signorina*— I cannot find them. I am afraid to search his pockets.'

Clare bit down on her impatience. 'Don't worry, Marco. I'll look myself.'

There was nothing in his pockets, Clare discovered, rigid with distaste. Then, as he turned his head restlessly, cursing and grumbling obscenities in his sleep, she heard a faint chink of metal and found the car keys under his pillow.

'*Avanti*,' she said quietly. 'I think he's coming out of it.'

She waited in agony as Marco, who insisted on driving, fumbled with the ignition and clashed the gears. As they moved off, bouncing down the dusty track, she thought she heard a shout from behind them, and saw that Marco had registered it too, that he was looking in the mirror and braking.

She said urgently, 'Keep going. I told you I'd look after you, and I will. But if you let me down, I'll throw you to the wolves.'

He sent her a miserable look, his forehead beaded with sweat, then obediently put his foot on the gas.

The track bordered fields of sunflowers for nearly a mile. The road, when they found it, was not much better, carving its way through scattered woodland and scrub. But Marco insisted they were going in the right direction.

Clare sat forward suddenly with a gasp. 'Oh, God. The Minerva. I—I forgot about it. Fabio still has it.'

'No, *signorina*. It is still in the boot of this car. Last night he wished only to celebrate—to get drunk—so he left it there.'

They were coming to a junction. Clare said cheerfully, 'Oh, dear. It just isn't his day...' And stopped with a gasp as a police car swung off the major road towards them, effectively blocking their passage.

'*Dio.*' Under his tan, Marco was as white as a sheet, as a second police vehicle followed. 'They are coming for me.'

'It's all right,' Clare soothed. 'Stop the car, and leave all the talking to me.'

But, with a sob of fright, he pulled the wheel over and swung the car off the road into the trees.

'Marco, this is crazy.' Clare tried to speak calmly. 'You can't drive in this. Now stop the car, and everything will be...' The words choked in her throat as Marco misjudged the distance between two trees and the offside crumpled on impact with a scream of grinding metal.

Clare was thrown forward, but her seat belt held. Marco, who wasn't wearing his belt, hit himself on the steering wheel and sat back, blood pouring from his nose and a cut on his head.

'Here.' She grabbed a handful of tissues from her bag,

and held them to his face as the police surrounded the car.

She thought hysterically, This can't be happening. It's like some ghastly action replay...

Her door was dragged open. She was aware of faces staring in at her. A babel of voices. Someone was asking her if she could move. She unfastened her seat belt and got out, steadying herself on the side of the car as the ground suddenly dipped and swayed.

Then the crowd around her were falling back, making way, and she saw Guido striding towards her, eyes blazing, face grim.

'You are hurt?' he demanded as he reached her, and curtly, over his shoulder, 'an ambulance—at once.'

She realised there was blood on her hands, and on the linen jacket, and tried to laugh feebly. 'Guido—it's not mine. It's poor Marco's...'

She got no further. He was looking past her to where Marco had just been pulled from the car, and there was an expression on his face Clare had never seen before—bleak—almost murderous.

He reached him in three strides, lifting the younger man as if he'd been a rag doll. Shaking him, his hands gripping his throat.

Clare moved then, pushing her way through, throwing herself at Guido, trying to drag him away.

'Don't—please don't hurt him. He helped me. I promised I'd make it all right for him.' She pummelled him with her fists. 'Guido—darling—let him go.'

'Are you mad?' His voice was hoarse. 'He collaborated with that piece of vermin. Why should I spare him?'

'Because he's your man.' There were tears running down her face. 'Because his father worked for you—and his grandfather before that. Because it's your land—your estate—and you are Bartaldi.'

Slowly Guido released his grip, and Marco slid to the ground at his feet, crimson-faced and choking.

'Yes, he's been a fool, and worse than a fool,' she went on quickly. 'But he's sorry, and I would never have got away without him. I gave my word that I'd look after him. That I wouldn't let him be arrested.'

'And what gives you the right to make such a dangerous promise?' His tone lashed her.

She looked up at him, longing to kiss the rigidity from his mouth. To smooth away the lines of strain from his dark face.

She said quietly, and very simply, 'Because I'm Bartaldi's woman. Now take me home—please.'

The silence was electric as he looked into her eyes, then he took her hand and raised it to his lips, before turning to the nearest policeman. 'Take the lady to my car, if you please, while I see what is to be done here.'

By the time he joined her reaction had set in, and she was shaking like a leaf. He gave her a frowning glance. 'I should take you to the hospital.'

'I hate hospitals,' she said. 'And I'll be fine.' She paused. 'Guido, you won't let them put poor Marco in jail, will you? His mother's sick, and he is one of your people…'

'You've made out your case, *mia cara*.' There was an odd note in his voice. 'I can refuse you nothing.'

She leaned back, closing her eyes, as the car moved smoothly forward. Well, the die was cast now. She'd offered herself, and he would take her. She supposed dully that he would buy her somewhere to live—an apartment in Rome, perhaps—and he would visit her there when he was able. She wasn't altogether sure how these arrangements worked.

But she did know that she could only ever occupy a small, separate part of his life, and she would have to make it enough.

She said, 'How did you know where to find me?'

'Ever since you told Tonio about "Marco's cousin" we have had Fabio watched. We thought Paola would be most in danger. I never once thought he would dare to touch you.

'When you disappeared last night, I thought at first that you had simply—left me. Then we found Violetta's car keys near the *campanile*, and realised the Minerva had gone too, and a sighting of Fabio's vehicle was reported.' He spoke quietly, without emotion. 'Marco was merely going to be picked up for interrogation.'

He paused. 'I hope you did not make any rash promises about helping Fabio to evade justice?'

'No,' she said. 'I hope they lock him up for ever.'

Then she remembered something completely different, and sat up. 'Guido—I should have told you—the Minerva—she's in the boot of that car.'

'Someone will find her and return her.'

'How can you be so casual about it?' Clare demanded indignantly. 'She's your greatest treasure.'

He said softly, 'Not any longer.' And, for one brief, tingling moment, his hand rested on her knee.

Everyone was clustered on the steps at the villa to witness their return.

Guido opened the passenger door and helped her out. Then, before she could move or protest, he picked her up in his arms and carried her up the steps.

In the sea of faces, the one she saw was Paola's, eyes

wide with shock and lips parted. And it brought her to her reeling senses.

'Guido—put me down,' she whispered. 'Are you crazy? What will people think?'

'What they wish, as usual,' he retorted without slackening his grasp, as he walked towards the stairs.

He carried her into her bedroom and put her gently down on the bed, then turned, beckoning to the housekeeper who had followed them, giving swift instructions that Clare barely heard.

A bath, deep and scented, was run for her, and Benedetta and Filumena were helping her to undress. She sank down into the water, boneless and weightless, and emerged to be wrapped in a warm bath sheet. Filumena dried her hair into a shining curtain, and Benedetta applied some sweet-smelling herbal ointment to the bump on her head.

The bed had been turned down, and there was even a nightgown waiting for her, one she'd never seen before, in ivory satin, with narrow straps and a deep plunge of a bodice made almost entirely of guipure lace. One side of the skirt was slashed almost to the thigh, and edged in the same lace.

She was suddenly aware of how deferentially they were treating her. And how their eyes slid away when she looked at them.

But what did she expect? By carrying her up the stairs like that Guido had put his mark on her. Virtually announced his intentions to the world.

She bit her lip. She could only imagine what Paola must be feeling, she thought with remorse.

The shutters were closed, reducing the room to discreet shadow, then Benedetta and Filumena withdrew with polite murmurs, and Clare was alone.

Or so she thought. But almost immediately the door opened, and Guido came in.

He had changed too, she saw, into slim-fitting black pants, that hugged his lean hips, and a black silk shirt. His face was serious, and a little remote.

'How do you feel?' He stood at the side of the bed and looked down at her.

'Much—better.' She hesitated, her eyes grave and a little disappointed. She'd expected him to behave with more finesse. 'You don't waste much time, *signore*..'

'Because I don't have much time to waste.' He paused in turn. 'Do you like the gown?'

'It's exquisite,' Clare returned with some of her old spark. 'Do you have a store of them—to meet all eventualities?'

'No.' He smiled at her. 'You have a lot to learn about me, *mia bella*.'

Her fingers plucked at the embroidered edge of the sheet. Her mouth felt suddenly dry. 'And is this going to be the first lesson?' Excitement warred with shyness inside her.

'That must wait a little, I think. Because we have to talk.' He sat down on the edge of the bed, and handed her a flat velvet case. 'I came to bring you this.'

It was a single diamond—a teardrop of fire on a slender gold chain.

'I searched for a flawless stone,' he went on. 'There is other jewellery, of course, some of it very old. But I wanted to give you something for yourself alone—something no one else had worn.'

She swallowed. 'It's the most beautiful thing I've ever seen. But you don't have to do this, Guido. I—I don't need jewellery or expensive presents. That's not it at all.'

'Then you will have to steel yourself, beloved. The

Marchesa Bartaldi is expected to wear the family jewels on grand occasions.'

She said woodenly, 'I'm sure Paola will look lovely. And don't you think you should be with her now?'

Guido fastened the pendant round her neck, adjusting the diamond so that it glittered in the valley between her lace-veiled breasts.

'The perfect setting,' he said softly. 'And is my company so undesirable, *mia cara*, that you wish to be rid of me?'

'No,' she said almost desperately. 'It's just that I want us to do the right thing—even though I know we're doing the wrong one. But I want us to do it as well as possible. And you're laughing at me.'

'Because you're talking nonsense.' He took her hands in his. 'Chiara—can you be the only person in the world who does not know I have come here to ask you to be my wife?'

She stared at him, her heart pounding suddenly, her lips parting on a soundless gasp. When she could speak, she said huskily, 'This is some joke. It—must be...'

'I have never been more serious.' He tapped his wristwatch. 'And I would like an answer, *carissima*. Every soul in the place is hanging on your word.'

'But you're going to marry Paola,' she protested wildly. 'She's in love with you. She told me so.'

'Then that will come as news to Tonio, to whom she's been engaged for the past forty-eight hours.'

'And you don't mind?' Her mind was reeling.

'It was what I always intended,' he said with a shrug. 'He has loved her for years, God help him. All that was needed was for Paola to stop falling for unsuitable men and realise she could only be happy with Tonio. Which she's now done.' He frowned swiftly. 'I thought she had told you.'

'She said something,' she returned numbly. 'But I didn't understand.' She shook her head. 'But why did you bring me here? You said you wanted me to make her into a willing wife for you...'

'No, my love. You were the one I always meant to have. And it was yourself that you had to coax into submission. Into acceptance of your fate. There were times when I thought it would never happen,' he added with feeling.

'Guido.' Her voice shook. 'You—*devil*.' She paused. 'But what about Paola's money? She said you didn't want it to go out of the company.'

'Paola has no money, *mia cara*, apart from the settlement I shall make on her when she marries. Her father gambled away everything he had. That was why my father took her into our home—because he felt that he should have stopped him years before.'

'And Tonio knows this?'

'*Naturalamente.*'

'Then why did you pretend that you were going to marry Paola?'

'To keep the undesirables away,' he returned promptly. 'Fabio was not the first, you understand. And she had to be protected while she learned the truth of her own feelings.' He smiled at her very tenderly. 'As you had to be, also, my stubborn darling. You were always so sure I wanted you to be my mistress. Whereas I simply wanted you.'

He paused. 'I am not a boy, Chiara, and you are not the first woman in my life. But you will be the last. And I know I am not the first man for you. Violetta has told me something of this James. Is there anything you wish to tell me too?'

'He's not important,' she said. 'He's been history for a long time. Only I thought you were like him—marrying for purely mercenary reasons. And it made me angry.'

'We have both had moments of doubt,' he said quietly. 'When I saw you on the station at Barezzo that day, I thought, Here she is at last. And then, when it seemed that you were Fabio's accomplice, I was angry too, and sick with disappointment.'

'You looked as if you wanted to kill me. When I saw you go for Marco today, I realised I'd had a lucky escape.'

'You've escaped nothing, *carissima*. Not unless you decide you don't want to marry me after all. That you don't love me.'

'I've loved you from the first, too,' she said. 'But I told myself I had to fight it.' She drew a breath. 'But there is something I have to know, Guido. The truth abut your lady in Siena.'

He was silent for a long moment. 'Her name is Bianca,' he said at last. 'And I knew her first about ten years ago. Yes, we were lovers—then. But we went our separate ways, and I did not meet her again until two years ago, when a mutual friend told me she was back in Siena, and very ill. And that she needed help.'

His mouth twisted. 'When I went to see her I found that she had contracted multiple sclerosis, and that it had advanced rapidly. She was married when her illness was diagnosed. Her husband could not take the idea of her disability, and walked out on her.

'I found her an apartment, and arranged for full-time care. The doctors tell me it will not be needed for very much longer. And I go to see her, and we laugh, and talk of old times, and I make sure that I treat her like the lively, beautiful girl I remember. Lately, I have told her about you,' he added quietly. 'And she has begged to meet you.'

'Oh, Guido.' Clare swallowed. 'I'm so sorry. And of course I'll come with you.' She shook her head. 'I've judged you so harshly. I don't understand how you can still want me.'

His smile teased her. 'But you know that I do.'

'Yes,' she said softly, her eyes luminous. 'I know.'

He leaned forward and kissed her, slowly and thoroughly, his mouth caressing hers with sensuous pleasure. And Clare, her arms round his neck, kissed him back, revelling in her freedom to do so. A freedom all the more precious for having been painfully bought.

And between kisses they murmured to each other, and laughed a little, and touched each other in delicate exploration.

At some point she found that Guido was now lying beside her, his silk shirt discarded, and that the straps of her nightgown had mysteriously slipped down, freeing her breasts from their little lace cups, and that he was stroking her excited nipples with the tip of a finger.

'You know how wrong this is, *mia bella*,' he whispered, his breath warm against her skin. 'Your godmother would be shocked. My uncle would be scandalised. I am supposed to wait patiently for our wedding night before I do this.' He bent and kissed each scented peak. 'Or this,' he added, his hand sliding under the slash of her skirt to find her moist silken core.

'Must we?' The breath caught in her throat as she arched against his caressing hand in mute demand. 'Wait, I mean?'

'I think we must.' His hand moved, subtly, wickedly, bringing a small moan from her throat. 'At least until I have locked the door and taken off the rest of my clothes.' He paused as his fingertips moved in devastating friction against her tiny centre of sensation. 'Or after—this.'

She came almost at once, her body pulsating in an eager delight that was close to pain, and he held her close, and kissed her mouth, and her tearful eyes, and murmured how beautiful she was, and how much he loved her.

And then he locked the door, and took off the rest of his clothes and her nightgown, and made slow, sensuous love to her, using his mouth and hands in ways she'd never dreamed of, enjoying her body in rapt completeness and teaching her to enjoy his.

'Tonight,' he said, when they were lying dreamily sated in each other's arms, 'I shall look at you at dinner and smile, and you will know what I am remembering. You—naked except for my diamond pendant.'

'This making it impossible for me to eat or drink anything.' Clare let her hand roam lazily. 'Anyway, I have my own memories, *signore*.' She looked at him from under her lashes. 'I suppose we shall have to remain celibate now until the ceremony.'

'I think we may also have to do penance,' he said ruefully. 'And apologise to all our well-wishers downstairs. I think my uncle and your godmother may be angry with us—unless they are too involved with each other to care.'

'Are they really fond of each other? That's wonderful.' She frowned a little. 'But Violetta has always vowed she would never get married again.'

'I think Cesare has other ideas. He will win her round. He saw at once that I loved you.'

'How clever of him.'

'We are a clever family, *carissima*' He turned her face to his and kissed her lingeringly. 'I think we should be married as soon as it can be arranged. Perhaps we had better not wait for the chapel to be finished.'

She smiled, pillowing her head on his chest. 'Are you in such a hurry, Marchese? I rather like being Bartaldi's woman.'

'You will find,' he said softly, 'that being Bartaldi's bride will be infinitely more rewarding.'

And as she walked down the aisle to Guido, waiting for her at the altar just a few brief weeks later, Clare saw the love in his face, and the pride, and the reverence. And she knew, joyously, that he was right.

Looking For More Romance?

Visit Romance.net

Look us up on-line at: http://www.romance.net

Check in daily for these and other exciting features:

Hot off the press

View all current titles, and purchase them on-line.

What do the stars have in store for you?

Horoscope

Hot deals

Exclusive offers available only at Romance.net

Plus, don't miss our interactive quizzes, contests and bonus gifts.

PWEB

HARLEQUIN® *Romance*®

Margot, Shelby and *Georgia*
are getting married. But first they have
a mystery to solve....

Join these three sisters on the way to the
altar in an exciting new trilogy from

BARBARA McMAHON

in Harlequin Romance

MARRYING MARGOT July 2000

A MOTHER FOR MOLLIE August 2000

GEORGIA'S GROOM September 2000

**Three sisters uncover secrets—
that lead to marriage with
the men of their dreams!**

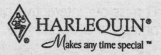

HARLEQUIN®
Makes any time special ™

HRBEAU

On sale October 2000

Forever Yours

You won't want to miss this
fabulous collection of
New York Times bestselling authors

BARBARA DELINSKY

CATHERINE COULTER

LINDA HOWARD

HARLEQUIN®
SUPERROMANCE®

You are now entering

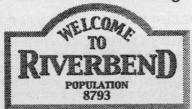

WELCOME TO **RIVERBEND**
POPULATION 8793

Riverbend...the kind of place where everyone knows
your name—and your business. Riverbend...home of
the River Rats—a group of small-town sons and
daughters who've been friends since high school.

The Rats are all grown up now. Living their lives and
learning that some days are good and some days
aren't—and that you can get through anything
as long as you have your friends.

Starting in July 2000, Harlequin Superromance brings
you Riverbend—six books about the River Rats and
the Midwest town they live in.

BIRTHRIGHT by Judith Arnold (July 2000)
THAT SUMMER THING by Pamela Bauer (August 2000)
HOMECOMING by Laura Abbot (September 2000)
LAST-MINUTE MARRIAGE by Marisa Carroll (October 2000)
A CHRISTMAS LEGACY by Kathryn Shay (November 2000)

Available wherever Harlequin books are sold.

HARLEQUIN®
Makes any time special ™

Coming Next Month

THE BEST HAS JUST GOTTEN BETTER!

#2121 THE ITALIAN'S REVENGE Michelle Reid
Vito Giordani had never forgiven Catherine for leaving, and now, seizing the advantage, he demanded that she return to Naples with him—as his wife. Their son would have his parents back together—and Vito would finally have…revenge!

#2122 THE PLEASURE KING'S BRIDE Emma Darcy
Fleeing from a dangerous situation, Christabel Valdez can't afford to fall in love. But she can't resist one night of passion with Jared King. And will one night be enough…?

#2123 HIS SECRETARY BRIDE
Kim Lawrence and Cathy Williams
(2-in-1 anthology)
From boardroom…to bedroom. What should you do if your boss is a gorgeous, sexy man and you simply can't resist him? Find out in these two lively, emotional short stories by talented rising stars Kim Lawrence and Cathy Williams.

#2124 OUTBACK MISTRESS Lindsay Armstrong
Ben had an accident on Olivia's property and had briefly lost his memory. Olivia couldn't deny the chemistry between them— but two vital discoveries turned her against him....

#2125 THE UNMARRIED FATHER Kathryn Ross
Melissa had agreed to pose as Mac's partner to help him secure a business contract. But after spending time with him and his adorable baby daughter, Melissa wished their deception could turn into reality....

#2126 RHYS'S REDEMPTION Anne McAllister
Rhys Wolfe would never risk his heart again. He cared about Mariah, but they were simply good friends. Their one night of passion had been a mistake. Only, now Mariah was pregnant— and Rhys had just nine months to learn to trust in love again.